OVER
THE RIVER AND
THROUGH
THE WOODS

Mindful Writers Retreat Series

Foreword by KATHLEEN SHOOP
Edited by DEMI STEVENS
Mindful Writers Retreat Authors

"Thanksgiving Traveler" – Janet McClintock
"Solstice" – Eileen Enwright Hodgetts
"Magic Sleigh Bed" – Michele Savaunah Zirkle
"Tidings of Comfort and Joyce" – Kimberly Kurth Gray
"The Bridge on the River Obi-Wan" – Ramona DeFelice Long
"Reminiscing on the Nostalgia of Happier Times" – Amy Morley
"Christmas Pearl" – Demi Stevens
"Once Upon a Life Well Spent" – Hilary Hauck
"The Christmas Tree" – Kathleen Shoop
"Tink" – Abigail Drake
"Limited Time Offer" – Phil Giunta
"Cranberry River" – Lorraine Donohue Bonzelet
"The Christmas Angel" – MaryAlice Meli
"A Gift" – Lori M. Jones
"Stars of Peace" – N.J. Hammer
"Fathers and Daughters" – Jennifer Diamond
"The Day the Magic Died" – James Robinson, Jr.
"Shaping Christmas" – Denise Weaver
"Buon Natale" – Cara Reinard
"First Nativity" – Larry Schardt
"'Twas a Hard Day's Night and Another Auld Lang Syne" – Sherren
    Elias Pensiero

Mindful Writers Retreat Series
135 Glen Avenue
Glen Rock, PA 17327

Print ISBN: 978-1-64649-191-9
Ebook ISBN: 978-1-64649-192-6

CONTENTS

FOREWORD

The winter holiday season provides a multitude of opportunities to mark the passing of time, observe religious, secular, and ethnic traditions, and share our hopes and dreams for the future with family, friends, and colleagues. We invite you to go *Over the River and Through the Woods* with us in a selection of short stories, poems, essays and recipes that celebrate all facets and depths of this yearly journey.

From Thanksgiving through New Year's, each piece gives a nod to the amazing swirl of jubilation and obligation that makes the time both magical and harrowing.

Thanksgiving is an American tradition that's been described and experienced as both holy and raucous. Historians like Samuel Eliot Morison (Reader's Digest) indicate that the first Thanksgiving was not only a time for thanks, "It was a three-day harvest festival that included drinking, gambling, athletic games..." The fourth Thursday of November allows people to gather, give thanks, and celebrate without the pressure of selecting and giving the perfect gifts. It's the ideal way to ring in the winter season with a sense of fun and gratefulness for all we have.

Trees and nature and the winter solstice have been revered since humans noticed the patterns of seasons and the enchantments each holds. Pagan revelry during dark winter stretches fed into Christians commemorating the birth of Jesus and all that his life meant in bringing joy and promise to the world. Hanukkah celebrates the Maccabee rebellion and the marvel of the menorah burning for eight days straight on one day's worth of oil. Kwanzaa celebrates African-American culture. New Year's Eve sends off the season with loud, sparkling parties that collapse with an exhale into the first day of the new year. This day provides a time to reflect, plan, and consider the kind of life a person wants to live going forward. And football. Football is threaded through each and every day of this marvelous season.

Like multi-colored, lighted evergreen swags, we've strung a literary collection that radiates a variety of reasons and ways people honor the winter holidays. Just like you might celebrate quietly on Christmas Eve, remembering your grandmother, or with a cymbal-crashing forty-person gathering on Christmas Day, these offerings allow you to gaze into firelit windows and see what others experience, to know how much we share as well as how we are different.

Over the River and Through the Woods fires up cooling love, questions faith, peeks into the mischief of elven magic, trusts that God will provide, and illustrates the wonder of the Christmas Tree tradition, holiday culinary delights, the belief in Santa and so much more. In addition to the delight that comes with the holidays, these stories call up conflicted emotions. Like you might gather with family for religious celebration and work associates to ring out the best fiscal year ever, this collection will provide a stocking-full of winter warmth. We invite you to light a fire, make your favorite hot drink, snuggle under a blanket and go over hill and dale into the most wonderful time of the year.

All proceeds from this collection will go to the Ligonier Camp and Conference Center, our location for the Mindful Writers Retreats. This lush Laurel Highlands center allows authors to gather to write, walk, and meditate. The experience results in enormous accomplishments as writers begin, muddle through, and finish projects. Its beautiful, peaceful setting fuels inspiration and provides the quiet needed to focus on the writing process. Woven throughout long writing days are the friendships and networks that grow and deepen beyond our retreat walls. Dozens and dozens of novels, poems, articles, essays, short-stories and more have been composed on these retreats.

The LCCC provides camp services to groups of all types and sizes all year long. Much of the work they do is geared toward children and their families. Because the center is priced reasonably, funding is important for them to maintain programming and housing. As we are always grateful to be welcomed back to the retreat center, we want to give back to its amazing staff and organization that make it all possible. We appreciate all they do for us, their bright smiles and open doors.

Thank you to all the authors who submitted to the collection. Thank you also to all who attend retreats and share the laughter, peace, and accomplishment that comes with writing with each other.

Thanks to Demi Stevens of Year of the Book Press for her editing, collaboration, cover design, and endless support. You have a librarian's eye for what is missing or is too much, and an editor's eye for all the rest—a priceless combination. Thank you two million times.

Thank you over and over to Wende Dikec, Lori Jones, and Kim Pierson for proofreading—you always find everything wrong... and I mean that in a good way.

Thanks to Julie Burns for your incredible attention to detail. You're a master proofer.

Thanks to Larry "Rock 'n' Roll" Schardt for helping make every retreat happen. So many little things, so much attention to all the bits that make the retreat seamless.

—Kathleen Shoop

THANKSGIVING TRAVELER

Janet McClintock

Kallie stepped onto the creaky porch and tucked the last of the firewood into the crook of her arm, praying it would hold out until the storm died down. She'd survived worse. But as soon as she thought it, she could almost hear the universe say, *"Oh yeah? Watch this."*

Her black and tan coonhound bayed into the wild, whipping snow. She turned toward the trail to the valley and shielded her eyes against the stinging snow pellets. "It's just the wind howling 'round the ridge, Roxie. Let's get inside out of the cold."

Before going through the door, she glanced over her shoulder for one last look into the swirling white. At first, it was a black dot that floated toward her, but it got bigger as it neared and formed into a black cowboy hat on a man hunched in his saddle, the collar of his long canvas duster pulled up over his ears. He rocked as his gray horse tramped through the snow, nose down, its long dark mane flapping in the wind.

"Hello-o," the man called out. He pulled his horse to a stop just short of the covered porch of Kallie's one-room cabin. "I got turned around in the storm and I saw your light."

"Where you headin'?" she asked, wishing she hadn't left the shotgun inside the door.

"Lone Wolf Ridge."

"You really wandered off the track," she said. "This is Bender Gap."

He held the brim of his hat against a violent wind gust. "You wouldn't have a fire and some hot coffee to warm a man up..."

No food. The last of the wood in her arms. The universe at work. But Kallie could not refuse help to a person in distress. "Go 'round back. I'll set this wood inside and meet you there. Get your horse settled in."

Her lean-to was set against a ridge and faced east where only the most determined snow swirled onto the straw bedding. Her sorrel mare, Russet, was already checking out the new arrival over the top rail of the fence. Kallie's stomach rumbled, and she worried about feeding the newcomer, but there was a bale of hay and sweet feed; at least the horses would eat.

She raised the lantern to see the man's face better, but at that moment he bent over to release the breast collar from the cinch. He wasn't especially tall, but his movements were efficient and agile. "Bring your saddle and bags inside," she said walking backward toward the feed shed, the wind blowing hard against her back and legs.

"I appreciate this, ma'am. And so does Dream Catcher," he yelled into the wind, patting the gray's neck.

She returned with two buckets of feed. The horses were going to have to get along overnight, and what better way to keep the peace than over food. They were herd animals and would be all right. The man had already released his horse into the paddock, and the two huffed their greetings. When they saw the buckets, they dove in as if forgetting they were strangers.

Kallie stared at the brand on Dream Catcher's dappled rump. Three crosses joined at the base. Curved crossbars formed an arc—the Triple Cross Ranch brand. Her stomach clenched, but not from hunger. "I put some extra corn in your horse's feed."

The man nodded and hoisted his saddle over one shoulder, saddlebags over the other. "It'll help keep him warm."

"Speaking of warm," Kallie said, rubbing her hands and blowing on them. "Let's get out of the cold."

When the man stepped inside, Roxie barked in long baying sounds, keeping her distance, but standing her ground.

"Roxie! It's okay." Kallie looked up at the stranger. "She's not usually like this."

The man dropped his gear inside the back door and stood with his hat in one hand; the other stroked a feather tucked into the band. "Pardon my manners, ma'am. I haven't properly introduced myself. I'm Michael Cunningham."

"Saw the Triple Cross brand. Figured you were a Cunningham. Just didn't know which one. I'm Kallie." She hooked her parka on the coatrack. "Kallie Bender."

"Is this a problem? Because I..."

"No. No problem. Hang your hat."

"I'm mighty thankful, ma'am."

Roxie sniffed toward Michael, still keeping her distance. She huffed and watched him over one shoulder on her way to her warm bed behind the cast iron stove.

A log popped and hissed. It was all the rustic cabin needed to fend off the cold—its warmth and the mellow light from two camping lanterns made the room homey.

"The couch is lumpy, but it's yours for the night if you want." Kallie stoked the fire and added a log. "I expected to close up the cabin and head back down the valley. One day tops, but this storm came out of nowhere. Can't offer you anything to eat. I already ate what little food I brought."

"I have plenty." He unpacked his saddlebags. "Nothing fancy, but it'll fill your gut." He piled canned beans, dried fruit, protein bars, and meat in white butcher's paper on the tiny kitchen counter. Fresh vegetables chopped and zipped into bags topped the pile.

Her stomach rumbled at the sight.

"I imagine the meat's still good, cold as it is out there," he said without looking up. "If you have water, I'll make coffee—French roast."

Her favorite. "You know, you're not so bad. For a Cunningham."

"No, ma'am." He smiled for the first time and a dimple curved around the corner of his mouth. She had expected a leathery, weather-carved face, but Michael's was smooth except for laugh lines and the dimple. His summer-blue eyes contrasted with dark eyelashes. Black Irish, her father had called the Cunninghams.

Michael finally said, "The water?"

"Oh, yes," she shook her mind into gear. "There's a pitcher on the counter."

"This empty one?" he asked, holding up a dented metal pitcher.

Her shoulders slumped and she exhaled. "I forgot. I was going to do that after I brought the wood in." She headed for her parka. "I'll get it now."

"I'll fetch it. Least I can do for your kind hospitality." He shrugged on his heavy coat.

"Off the front porch, turn left. About thirty feet there's a handpump." She grabbed two more pitchers and handed them to him. "No sense going out in the storm more than you have to."

He tugged his hat onto his head. "No, ma'am."

Roxie got up from her warm spot to stand next to Kallie in the doorway and watch Michael cross the yard, leaning into the wind, holding his hat on his head. The storm snapped his duster's flaps behind him.

Roxie woofed.

"Yeah, I know he's a Cunningham. But we can't throw him out into this storm."

Roxie emitted a whiny yawn and licked her silver-flecked chops.

"It's only one night, ol' girl."

Michael headed back still holding onto his hat, three full pitchers in one strong hand. He passed them to her and stomped the snow off his boots. "Use this wisely. I think your pump's getting ready to freeze up on you."

An hour and a half later, Michael's spoon clanked in his empty bowl, and he pushed back from the table. "At least your stomach stopped growling."

Kallie put a finger to her lips until she swallowed the food in her mouth. "You heard it?"

He grinned. "I heard it a half a mile away through the storm."

"Oh, you did not," she said. A Cunningham with a sense of humor—must be a *distant* relative.

They hadn't talked while she made the stew and he brewed the coffee. Dinner conversation had only consisted of "Pass me the salt" or "More coffee?" They had an hour or so until bedtime. What would a Bender have to say to a Cunningham?

The silence pressed on them, then they both spoke at once. They urged each other to begin until Michael finally said, "You're the hostess. You start."

Kallie cleared her throat. Might as well start with the question that had bothered her all evening. "I have to admit, I never paid much mind to the Cunninghams, but I don't remember a Michael. Which one are you?"

He looked at her through those dark lashes. "I'm from out of town. I'm at the Triple Cross for the holidays."

"What'll you be doing?"

He broke off a piece of dark bread and swiped gravy off the bottom of his bowl. "Just here to help out." He glanced up. "With Tyler gone and all."

"Of all the Cunninghams, Tyler was the nicest. But still..." Kallie frowned. "He got a full-ride football scholarship like his brothers before him, while me and my brothers paid our way through college, racking up debt." Her father's words filled her head: *"Those who have get."*

"Sounds like you hold a grudge," Michael said.

"Not really. Not anymore. There's a certain peace in letting go of ill will." She shrugged. "It can be an anchor, if you let it."

Michael sat back, watching her as if looking past her tough exterior. "Tyler never got to use the scholarship. He died in an accident three months ago."

"I heard and I'm sorry for your loss," she said. "I apologize for not sayin' it earlier."

"No need to apologize. A bad storm gets everybody a little discombobulated."

She snorted a laugh and stood to clear the table. "Discombobulated?" With one word, he had softened the heaviness between them.

"What word would you use?" He helped carry the dirty dishes to the sink.

"Never really thought about it." She grabbed the kettle off the wood stove and poured hot water into two basins, squeezing dish soap into one, then set about cleaning the dishes. "I guess a storm makes us revert to our survival instincts. Gotta be ready for it."

"When I got here, you had no food, very little wood, and no readily available water. You didn't seem too ready."

She looked out the window into the darkness. Somewhere there was almost a full moon, but clouds shrouded the ridge, blocking the moon and holding the darkness captive. She refocused on her reflection in the windowpanes. "I was psyching myself up to endure it until the first day I could ride out of here. A person can go a long time without food."

Michael's reflection showed him looking directly at her. "You weren't concerned?"

"I'm used to struggling." She scoured a pot. "I'm a Bender."

"That you are." He took the soapy pot from her and dunked it into the clear water before setting it on the drainer.

"How would you know?" she asked. "You're not from around here."

"The Bender legend is alive and well in the Cunningham clan. Tough outdoorsmen, excellent marksmen, strong-willed—"

"By that you mean stubborn."

"You say 'stubborn'. We say 'strong-willed'." He poured the last of the coffee into two mugs. "My turn to ask a question."

"Shoot." She dumped the water and wiped out the basins.

"I was never clear on the feud between the two families."

She draped the towel over the sink edge and straightened it, waiting for the question behind that statement. A log dropped in the fire and the hissing intensified. Michael went to the stove and poked at the embers before adding a log. The fire roared and Kallie slipped into one of the rockers to warm her feet.

Wiping his hands on his pantlegs, he asked, "Do you know what the feud's about?"

"From what I understand, Angus Cunningham offered my great-grandfather, C.J. Bender, the opportunity to share acreage for our cattle. It was a boon for us. More range meant more cattle. More cattle meant more revenue." Kallie rocked and thought.

"I hear a 'but' coming."

She nodded, her gaze intent on the stove. "But something happened, and Angus felt C.J. was ungrateful. He pulled the offer. C.J. had all these cattle and no place for them to graze. Had to dump them at below-market. Guess who bought 'em up."

"Angus." Michael's voice was barely audible. "Do you know what happened to make him change his mind?"

"No. C.J. couldn't come to any other conclusion than he was set up. It took the Bender Ranch a long time to recover financially. It's still touch and go."

"You know the families today had nothing to do with that, right?"

"It's not that simple."

"It's not complex." After a pause, he continued. "It's the night before Thanksgiving. Why come up here now?"

"My brothers turned the ranch over to me. Times are tough, and..." She rubbed her forehead. "I'm thinking about selling it."

"Selling your homestead." Michael exhaled slowly. "Do you think you will?"

"Not sure. I had to get away to clear my head. Had to close this place up for the winter anyway." She pulled on her boots. They were warm inside from the stove.

"Where are you going?"

"I'm getting sleepy and I better bed down the horses while my eyes are still open."

"I'll give you a hand." He pulled on his boots, stood, and stretched.

There was no need to worry. The two horses stood side by side sharing body heat in the back of the lean-to where the wind barely ruffled their tails. While Kallie broke open the hay bale and tossed a couple of sections over the railing, Michael broke the glaze of ice on the water trough, and Roxie sniffed around taking care of her business for the night.

Kallie leaned on the split-rail fence and watched the horses. Strangers. Nose to tail like old friends. Michael joined her, putting a foot on the lower rail. Roxie nosed Kallie's arm. The wind stopped, and their breath vapor floated in front of their faces. It was so quiet they could hear the snowflakes pattering around them. The universe could be serene... at times.

"There's a peacefulness about you," Michael said. "You don't want me here, but you're hospitable. Why don't you extend that to the Cunningham clan?"

"Why don't *they* step up?"

After a brief silence, he said, "When there is no peace around you, share yours."

A wind gust made Michael grab his hat.

"Br-r," she said. "Let's get back to the warm cabin."

Back inside, another log on the fire, boots resting beside the stove, Michael said, "I have one cocoa packet left. Would you like to share?"

"You enjoy it."

They sat rocking in front of the fire, Michael sipping his cocoa, Kallie lost in thought. He reached over, offering the hot cocoa to her, and without thinking, she took it. It was rich and sweet.

She handed it back to him. "You talk different."

"I'm not from around here."

She *humphed* a short chuckle. That was an understatement. He wasn't a local Cunningham; any conversation with them was harsh and abrupt. She thought about what Michael said outside. "Why haven't the Cunninghams extended the olive branch?"

"Maybe they don't know how, or they're waiting for a Bender to step over the line and make peace."

She shook her head. "Three generations of back-stabbing and hatefulness."

"Over something no one alive today is responsible for."

"It's just one of those things." She knelt in front of the stove, added the last log, and banked the fire for the night. "I'm going to bed. You'll be okay on the couch?"

He smiled. "My bedroll is all I need."

She turned off the lanterns, disrobed to her thermal underwear, and crawled under the wool blankets. Michael's preparations made light swishing noises while Roxie made two circles and dropped back onto her bed with a thud.

"Kallie?"

"Yeah."

"Tomorrow's Thanksgiving. What are you thankful for?"

"Hadn't much thought about it." What was she thankful for? Life. Family. Health. Those went without saying. "What about you?"

"I'm thankful you took me in," he said without hesitation.

"Me, too."

"After seeing that all Cunninghams aren't bad, do you think you might be the one to cross the line?"

"You got me thinkin' about it."

"Sweet dreams, Kallie."

Kallie stuck her head out from under the covers and opened one eye. And quickly closed it. The sun streamed through the windows, lighting up the entire one-room cabin.

"Michael? You awake?"

No answer.

She pushed down the covers and squinted across the room. The cabin was empty. She twisted around to check for his gear. Nothing. She raced to the back door only to see Russet looking over the railing toward the house, waiting for her breakfast. Roxie nuzzled Kallie's hand.

"There's a Cunningham for ya," she said to the aging hound, rubbing her long, velvety ears. "Leaves without so much as a goodbye."

She slid into yesterday's clothes and motioned for Roxie to follow her. "What do ya say, we get Russet taken care of?"

Without the cloud cover, the air was crisp and clear. Fresh snow glistened in the sunshine. Russet whinnied a good morning when Kallie scratched her jaw and looked past her. "You ponies ate *all* that hay? Didja turn into hogs overnight?" she joked with a final scratch before heading to the feed shed.

She stopped in the doorway. The feed shed felt different. She stilled, only moving her eyes until they fell on the hay. The bale she'd opened last night had unbroken twine. No hay was missing. Russet whinnied and banged a hoof against a fence pole.

Kallie shivered and pulled her knife from her pocket to cut the twine. "Hold on, Russet. Breakfast is coming."

After tossing a couple of sections of hay over the rail, she hung Russet's feed bucket on its hook. She looked for Dream Catcher's hoofprints to see which way Michael had gone, but the only indentations in the snow were hers and Roxie's. Must have left before the storm stopped, or, more likely, she had dreamed about a pleasant Cunningham, because how real was that?

Roxie bayed from the back steps.

"Coming." Kallie patted the dog's head on her way past.

Now that she was awake and back inside, the cabin had the same strangeness as the feed shed. She stood inside the back door and scanned the room. Something didn't ring true. She wandered through the room trying to figure out what else was amiss, and her gaze fell on the shelf. No food, no leftovers. The empty drainer troubled her, heightening her senses. The roof creaked from a wind gust.

Roxie snuffled at something on the floor.

"Whatcha got, girl?" Kallie took a feather from the hound's mouth and turned it over in her hand. It looked like the one from the traveler's hat. She studied the feather—it had survived the blasts of wind and icy snow only to fall out in her house. That was one heck of a dream.

She opened the front door and squinted from the brightness. The undisturbed drifts in the path to the valley sparkled in the sunlight. The traveler had ridden in on the storm and took it with him when he left. Grateful that he had got her thinking about a resolution to the family feud, it bothered her that she couldn't tell him how much it meant or, more importantly, return the favor. As she rubbed the feather across her cheek, she inhaled deeply, relishing the clean mountain air as it filled her lungs, expanding them. The warm cabin called to her, but she didn't want to turn her back on the new day.

She thought of the conversation the night before when the traveler had talked about peace. After several more seconds enjoying the Thanksgiving morning freshness, a smile dawned on her face. The universe had not made her suffer, but instead had cleared her head, helping her see what she had to do—keep the ranch and reconcile with the Cunninghams.

"Think you're great?" She pointed the feather at the universe. "Watch this."

SOLSTICE

Eileen Enwright Hodgetts

The neon sign flickers. Its intermittent red light cuts through the cold mist that rises from the river and creeps past derelict buildings. Life has gone from here along with the mills, the train tracks, and the huddled houses, but Lou's Place remains. His neon L has lost the will to shine and the apostrophe makes only an occasional contribution. It doesn't matter. I know where I am, but why am I here?

I park beneath the flickering light and take my purse from the front seat. I open the car door and step out into cold night air that smells of mold, rust, river water and a hint of burning tires; in other words, nothing has changed.

When I reach the curb I turn to remotely lock the car. This is a nice sturdy Ford Escape, and it doesn't belong in this neighborhood. I should set the alarm, and yet... no, I will not. When I was an art student driving a rusted PT Cruiser, I would never have locked the doors here. I may not be that girl now but remnants of her lurk in the dark places of my soul, refusing to lock the car. It's a small gesture of defiance, one my husband would not understand. But Jay is not here... and he will never know.

I glance up and down the street seeing only the long, low shape of an old black Cadillac and the hulking presence of a tricked out monster truck, its chrome reflecting the wounded flicker of the neon sign. Nothing moves, not even a rat. This is the shortest night of the year—the winter solstice—and somewhere else in the world people are dancing naked around blazing bonfires, but here in the rusted valley of the dead steel industry, nothing moves.

I push open the door to the bar. Mist trails me, smelling faintly of smoke as it wraps itself around my feet and slithers inside. My uncomfortable high-heeled shoes stick to the floor. Lou has never been much for mopping and sweeping. I welcome the familiarity just as I welcome the odor of stale beer and overused cooking oil. This place—Lou's Place—is my place and I have been gone too long.

Lou is behind the bar, of course. I watch his face and wait for recognition. His eyes, burrowed among rolls of fat, gleam contentedly and his face lights up in a wide, knowing grin.

"Amy!"

"Lou."

"Where have you been?"

I should know how to answer that question. I've graduated; I've married; I have a job; I am wearing a suit. I am not the Amy he remembers, and yet I am here.

Lou dismisses my silence with a wave of a large hand. "Have a drink, on the house. Celebrate the solstice. Rum and Coke, right?"

"Just the Coke."

He raises his eyebrows. "You used to drink."

"I used to shave my head and make pictures out of dryer lint," I reply.

He grins, remembering.

"I'm driving," I say. "I came in to use your phone. Seems you don't have a cell signal here."

Lou laughs. "We're lucky we have electricity."

"But you still have a land line?"

He gestures with his head toward the back room where I can hear voices and the click of pool cues. "On the wall back there. Darned if I know why it's still working. It's not like I ever pay the bill. You go ahead. I'll bring your drink. Don't worry about them."

"Don't worry about who?"

"The two guys playing pool. Don't worry about them." He lowers his head and I can barely make out his whispered words. "They'll change you."

"What?"

"Nothing. Go ahead. Make your call. Husband?"

"Yeah. I have to tell him I'll be late."

Lou glances at the watch embedded in the roll of fat at his wrist. "You'll miss *Jeopardy*."

Yes, I will, and Jay will be annoyed because he likes us to watch it together, but I can't let Lou know. I can't reveal what I have become.

"I don't watch *Jeopardy*," I lie.

Lou grins. "I do."

As I turn toward the back room I can't help wondering how Lou manages to get a television signal down here in the abandoned valley.

I have another question, one that I don't want to ask myself. *Why am I down here using Lou's phone?* All I have to do to find a cell signal is drive up out of the valley to the suburbs where the lights shine and life is predictable. I could have called Jay from anywhere, so why did I come here?

Two men are playing pool in the back room. I remember Lou's whispered words. *"They'll change you."* I don't want to change. I give them a quick glance wondering which one came in the Cadillac. One man is short with a halo of red curly hair. Perhaps he drives the monster truck to compensate for his lack of height. The other man is tall with black hair falling in waves to his shoulders. His dark overcoat is more suited to a downtown law firm than a derelict bar. He meets my eyes as I pass and I feel a stab of emotion. Recognition? No, I have never seen him before. Empathy? His dark eyes are shadowed and sad. Something is very wrong.

The short man tugs at his sleeve. "Hey come on, Mario. It's still your turn."

Mario is looking at me. "I'm finished, Marty."

"No, you ain't."

Mario turns away from me. "I'm done, Marty. I can't play. I've lost another one."

Marty groans. "Where?"

"On the floor somewhere."

I hear footsteps behind me and see Lou approaching with a can of Coke and a glass. The glass is a nice touch, but I find it insulting. Who does he think I've become?

"Watch out for the tall one," Lou says softly. He sets the glass on a table near the wall phone. "Make your call, Amy... if you can."

I snatch up the phone and feel a wave of relief as I hear a dial tone. Well, what did I expect? I'm not a prisoner here. I can leave at any time. My car is outside. I dial and am rewarded with a message telling me to wait for the beep. Nothing wrong with that, I tell myself. Jay is probably talking to his mother, or his sister, probably complaining that I'm late home. I leave a message for him to call me back. I read the number from a sticker beside the phone. "Call me. I'll explain." Really? Do I even have an explanation?

I sit at the table and pour Coke into the glass.

Marty is on his knees searching for something under the pool table. Mario stands, holding the pool cue, his dark eyes focused on nothing. *The tall one!* What about the tall one?

Marty scrambles to his feet with a shout of triumph. "I found it."

Mario looks at him with only a flicker of interest before he turns his attention to me. He smiles, a flash of white teeth in a lean handsome face. "Hi," he says.

"Hi," I reply.

"Oh come on, Mario," Marty says. "Don't start anything. You know what happens."

Mario is still smiling, but it's not a happy smile. "Shortest day of the year," he says in a conversational tone. "Winter solstice."

"Yes, winter solstice," I reply as though I am repeating a formula, or a liturgical greeting.

"Don't do it, Mario," Marty says. He capers toward me monkeylike, and drops something into my glass. "Here lady, stir your drink."

My Coke foams for a moment. I stare down into the glass. What has he put in there? I'm sure as anything not going to drink it, whatever it is.

"Please," Mario says in a choked voice. "Please, don't look."

He's too late. I have already looked. For some reason Marty has dropped a fake joke finger into my drink. No, it's not fake! It's a real finger. I jump up, flinging my hand out and knocking the glass over onto the table.

There it is, lying in a pool of brown liquid, a small, pink finger.

I dance from one foot to the other screaming out, "Oh my God! Oh my God. Lou!"

Mario towers beside me, his face flushed with anger or embarrassment. His voice is cold. "Pick it up, Marty."

Marty replies with a cackling laugh. "It won't hurt her."

I am still stammering and looking around for the owner. "Lou, Lou." I look down at the table. There is no doubt about it. "It's a finger," I stutter.

Lou has not appeared yet but Mario has overcome his embarrassment and bows slightly to me. "Please forgive my friend. He has no manners. Let me remove this... object."

He extends his hand and I am seized with the impossible realization that the finger on the table has come from Mario's hand and now he has only a thumb and a little finger. There is no blood and no sign of trauma... but three of his fingers are missing.

I wait in agonized, embarrassed silence while he chases the finger around the table attempting to grasp it.

He speaks softly. "I'm sorry about this."

"So am I," I say.

At last he manages to slide the finger to the edge of the table where he pushes it into the pocket of his overcoat.

Marty is cackling again. "Neat, ain't it? It don't hurt him a bit, and he don't bleed."

Mario aims a kick at his companion's ankle, sending him hopping away from the table. "Be quiet, Marty. You're bothering the lady. We really should leave."

Yes, you should, I think. Or maybe I should be the one to leave. But I don't, and neither does Mario. He sits at the table and gives me another inviting smile. I remain standing, my feet glued to the floor—but this time it is not the grime that holds me.

Mario looks past me and I turn to see Lou hovering in the doorway. "Lou," Mario says, "please bring the lady another drink. She spilled hers."

"Yeah," says Lou. "I saw what happened. You want another, Amy, while you're waiting for your phone call?"

My phone call! I shake my head. "No, Lou. No more Coke."

Mario smiles again. "Please, sit... *Amy.*"

I shake my head again. I cannot sit.

Marty is beside me, grinning. "You should sit next to him, lady. It ain't catching. I pick 'em up for him all the time. He don't always know when he's dropped one. They grow back."

Mario's stare is intense. "They used to," he says. "Please Amy, you should sit down. You're looking very pale. There is no need to be afraid. I don't bite." He smiles ruefully. "I don't even pinch... not anymore."

"It's only fingers," Marty says.

I take a deep breath and finally manage to move my feet. Stumbling to a chair, I sit across from Mario. Marty grabs Mario's left hand and thrusts it in my face. "Look, he's growing new ones on this hand."

I breathe deeply and try to focus. Mario's hand has the required number of digits, but they are tiny, like baby fingers.

Mario snatches his hand away. "No. They've stopped growing. I knew this would happen. No point in pretending."

A worried scowl creases Marty's face. "Shit man, don't say that. Don't say nothing like that."

I ask the obvious question. "Have you seen a doctor?" I am ashamed of the question as soon as I ask it.

Marty pulls up a chair and leans his elbows on the table. "Doctors? Shitheads!"

"I've seen doctors," Mario says.

A meaty hand reaches down beside my shoulder and sets a glass on the table. "Rum and Coke," Lou says, "to settle your mind."

"My mind is fine," I say, but I take the drink.

"You want me to get rid of them?" Lou asks. "It's not too late. Not yet."

Not too late for what? I wonder. I look at the phone. "I need to talk to my husband," I say. "That's why I came."

Mario's eyes are dark and pained. "There was no need for that."

"I don't know what you mean."

"You didn't have to drag your husband into this. I'm not going to hurt you. You don't need his protection."

I start to protest. "I wasn't..." Wasn't what? What was I doing? Why was I here? Why didn't I just drive out of the valley? I didn't need to wait for Jay's call. I could just go home, and forget all about this, whatever this is.

Lou folds his arms and glares at Marty. "This ain't about you," he says. "So you stay out of it and don't do nothing weird. It's all under control."

Marty rises, spluttering indignantly. "Screw you. I ain't the weird one. I got all my body parts."

Lou raises a warning finger, shakes his head at Marty and turns back to the bar.

Mario is talking to me. "So, you have a husband?"

"Yes."

That is really all that I want to say about Jay. He's not important; not here.

The silence stretches into a long uncomfortable moment. I want to ask Mario, but asking will make everything real—the terrible sadness in his eyes, the vulnerability of his deformed left hand, the puddle of Coke and the... *thing*... he slipped into his pocket. If I say nothing, perhaps it will not exist, but I cannot allow the silence to continue.

My voice sounds cold. "This... er... condition of yours... have you had it long?"

"Long enough." Mario's eyes are focused on my rum and Coke. He needs a drink; I don't blame him. I push the glass toward him. "Go ahead, take it," I say. "I don't want it."

Mario stares at the glass. "No, I don't suppose you do. You'll never look at a Coke the same way again, will you?"

I am mesmerized. I cannot move from my seat; I can only speak to the beautiful, sad man beside me. "It wasn't your fault," I say. "Go ahead, take it."

"I can't."

"Yes, you can. I don't want it and..." I am stupid, thoughtless, ashamed of myself. "I'm sorry. You can't, can you? Do you need a straw?"

"Forget it. I don't want it."

"Why did it happen," I ask, "this thing with your fingers?"

"I don't know. Perhaps it's a curse."

I've run out of words again. I fold my hands in my lap, knitting my fingers together as though I am afraid of losing them. I feel for my thumbs, my ring finger with its wedding band, my little finger where I wear my grandmother's ring. The smoke that I brought with me from outside still lingers, now fogging my view of the telephone. *Why doesn't Jay call me back?*

"Isn't there someone who can help you?" I ask, although I don't know what I'm really suggesting.

Marty is back, glowering at me from behind Mario's chair. "Butt out, lady. I'm helping him."

"I meant professional help."

"He don't want no professional help," Marty says. "Just his family."

"I thought it would go away, but it didn't," Mario says.

"So," says Marty, "finally he comes to me 'cause I'm his cousin and he don't wanna be seen no more in the city. I tell him there ain't nobody he knows gonna see him on Mill Front Street. Ain't no one gonna go looking for Mario Amelio, Esquire, not here."

"Esquire?" I ask. "You're a lawyer."

"I was a lawyer."

Marty pats him on the back. "He was slick, the brains of the family. There ain't no one done better than my cousin Mario. He didn't used to have nothing to do with me. Mr. Big Shot, he was. We was the poor relations. It ain't the same now. He don't have no one else no more."

Mario looks down at his hand. "They're not growing back. Not this time."

I want to touch him. I want to hold his ruined hands and let him know I am not afraid. But I can't move. I can't even unlace my fingers. I feel as though I will lose them if I don't hold onto them. "Give 'em time, Mario."

"I've given them time," Mario says, standing up and pushing back the chair. "What's next? Toes? Ears? The obvious?"

I know what he means. I don't need Marty to clutch his crotch and roll his eyes dramatically.

"I'm sorry," I say. "It must be very difficult for you." It's a stupid remark, banal and obvious.

"It's not what I was expecting," Mario says. "I had it all once. I lost it."

I think of my Ford Escape, my house in the suburbs, my husband who will record *Jeopardy* and wait for me to come home. I try not to think of the artwork I keep in the basement—the paintings made with gunpowder, the collage of multicolored dryer lint, the girl with the shaved head who ate a macrobiotic diet. That girl no longer exists.

"I don't want to lose what I have," I say.

"Of course not."

I struggle for words. "It's not personal. It's nothing to do with your..."

Marty is back. He is wrapped in a down jacket many sizes too big and he wears a knitted hat with strings hanging down like schoolgirl braids. He jerks his head at Mario. "Come on, man, let's go if we're going. The fire's already lit."

Fire? I remember the smoke and the smell of burning tires, and my sudden random thought of winter solstice. Somewhere people are dancing naked around a bonfire. I shudder. I cannot imagine Marty naked, and I refuse to imagine Mario.

I watch them leave, Marty still capering monkeylike, Mario tall and graceful. I pick up my drink and walk across to the bar where Lou is wiping glasses with a ragged cloth.

"I'm ashamed of myself," I say.

He continues to wipe. "No need."

"I wasn't very accepting."

"It ain't easy."

I take a guess and jump off the cliff. "You wanted me to come here tonight."

"Did I?"

"You called me. I don't know how, but you called me."

"You were in danger."

"Of what?"

"Of losing yourself."

"No, I'm fine. I'm perfectly fine."

"But you came."

I have nothing to say.

Lou polishes a glass. He does not look at me. "There were sparks, Amy."

"There's something wrong with him."

"There's something wrong with all of us."

"But not like that."

"It ain't always that easy to see."

The phone is ringing. I turn my head; Jay is calling back.

Lou raises his voice above the jangling phone. "Over by the door. He dropped something. If you pick it up you'll..."

The phone is still ringing. "I'll what?" I ask.

Lou says nothing. I walk to the door and see what Mario dropped. It's small and pink—a baby finger. I pick it up and it moves. It curls and clutches my ring finger. The door opens and I see Mario framed in the doorway wreathed in smoke. The phone jangles.

I look up at Mario. "Let go of me, please. I have to answer the phone."

"I'm not holding you," he says.

The phone stops ringing. Lou is speaking. "Amy? No there's no one here called Amy."

"I'm here," I shout. "I'm still here."

Lou walks toward me with a heavy tread. "You're not here," he says. "Not the Amy you used to be. You made a choice. "

I'm angry now, with Lou, with the idea that I can go back to being the girl I used to be, with the smoke pouring through the doorway, and with the idea that I can be held in place by Mario's tiny finger. I flick my hand and shake myself free. The finger flies away into the darkness.

I am suddenly glad I didn't lock the car. I fling open the door and lock myself inside while I fumble for my keys. Driving up and out of the dead valley where the shadows of rusted mills dance in the firelight, I do not stop until the Christmas lights of suburbia outshine the solstice bonfires.

And while I drive, I count my fingers. So far, so good.

MAGIC SLEIGH BED

Michele Savaunah Zirkle

Ciara raised her arms high in sun salutation, her hopes rising with them. She would heal, she told herself. People get divorced every day. They move on. They eat and sleep, laugh and play. They live. They breathe and sometimes, if they are a lucky Irish girl like herself, they find another soul-mate.

She peered out the window of the yoga studio. The glowing green sign above the pub across the street cast an outline of a shamrock onto her feet. Must everything Irish remind her of him—of his impish grin—his tousled hair that, in the right light reflects the slightest red?

A tear fell to her mat and she teetered in her one-legged tree pose as the three-pronged symbol blurred. She would love again. Maybe not the exact same way she'd loved Art, but she had to believe that God was good and would plug the hole in her heart.

She wagged her tail in downward dog, resisting the urge to bark. If she were a canine, she could bite the man who had taken off to Japan on business and never returned to walk her down the aisle. All those chats over dinner about the future they envisioned—the last on Valentine's Day, the same day he had proposed to her over a Guinness and fries.

The proposal hadn't shocked her, but her intense feelings for him after only five months of dating had. Climbing into his truck, holding his hand, sipping from his coffee mug. Everything about him had been comfortable. A peculiar comfortable that she felt could be due to having spent another lifetime together.

Her voice sounded familiar, he'd said during their first call after connecting on the hip online dating site. The cold, dreary days of December seemed a bit warmer with the casual chatter occupying her mind and coffee filling her mug.

She held tight in plank position, her blonde hair dangling. Yoga reminded her of evenings at class when Art was in town. She'd like to have just one of those evenings back. She'd make dinner and write her novel until he finished emailing and graphing the company's growth. Then, moonlight streaming, she'd lay nestled in his arms on the patio chair as he pointed out the Jupiter-Venus-Mars trine and speculate on the possibility of life on other planets.

He had to miss that, too. He had to miss her kiss, her odd sense of humor, and especially her company on a random business trip. She had managed to make time to travel with him. They had that in common. Merrimon Hotels were home away from home for the nomad in them both, but exploring the world side by side wasn't enough to keep them together.

Lying on her back in Shivas Ana, flute music playing, she reflected that life wasn't fair. Love wasn't fair. So, why was she expecting God to be fair? Nothing made sense anymore. Absolutely nothing.

"Namaste," the yoga instructor said, bowing.

"Namaste," Ciara said, relieved to feel at one with the universe even for the moment.

Ciara tightened the scarf around her neck and strolled past the second-hand bookstore-hangout for yogis and want-to-be authors guzzling coffee as fast as the plotlines spinning in their heads. She propped her well-worn yoga mat against the frozen bench under the gazebo in the town square and was tracing the flight of a pigeon when her cell buzzed.

"Can you meet me at your place in a few? I can pick up the bed," said her brother Matt.

"Sure," Ciara said, hopping up and jogging to her car.

A few miles later she pulled in front of her rented brownstone where Matt waited, tailgate down.

She wrapped her arms around him and breathed in the sweet smell of cedar.

He rubbed her back. "Wish I could fix the bed, but I just cut down the trees, you know."

"Yep," Ciara said, opening the front door. "Grandma thinks if I have love that it will magically find me like it did her and Grandpa, but she's old school. Doesn't know the real secret is that we create our own reality, not some bear."

Matt walked toward her squinting as if he could gauge his next comment by doing so. "Heard from him?"

Ciara snarled. "I don't talk to dead people."

"Not Grandpa," Matt said, pressing his knuckles gently against her cheek. "Art."

She slid away. "Not for months. Only talked to him a few times after he left for Japan. Guess he got himself a Geisha girl." She picked up a wooden knob from the floor and stroked the broken bedpost leaning against the wall of the foyer.

Matt placed a calloused hand on her shoulder. "You know what happened to Scrooge in his bed, right? Any man who chooses business over love will regret it. Maybe even get the shit scared out of him by a group of chain-wearing spirits who make him pee the bed."

Ciara imagined Art's terrified face and smiled. "Maybe his bed is haunted, but mine isn't."

Matt laughed.

Ciara wrinkled her nose. "I like sleeping in my own bed."

Matt winked. "Grandma insisted you get this one when she transferred to the senior community. Too bad the movers broke it, but if anyone can fix this beauty, Tim can," he said, hoisting the sleigh-sloped headboard off the ground as if deadlifting for a championship.

Ciara smiled and waved the knob. "I got this. No worries!"

That night Ciara snuggled into the supple homemade quilt and watched through the bedroom window as snow dripped like feathers. She fell into a deep sleep.

By the time morning light seeped into the room, Ciara was petting the pillow, a crusty memory of happiness swirling in her head. She labored to open her eyes, lumbered up, got dressed and headed to work at Rock Garden State Park.

On her way, she soaked in the glorious remnants of snow dusting the rooftops and stopped at the Latte Lounge where she overheard an older couple behind her in line talking about a bear sighting in town.

"Not that unusual here," the barista with braided hair behind the counter said. "Rare to see the cubs though."

"Americano. Medium," I said, scratching my forehead and turning to the couple. "When did you see a bear?"

"Oh, we didn't," the silver-haired lady replied, patting the man's arm. "We overheard it from our great-grandson's teachers at school drop-off this morning, but it sounds like a ton of people near the town square saw it."

"An impromptu appearance could make the Christmas Parade interesting," she said, the image of the bear engraved on the broken antique bed her grandfather made flashing between her and the aroma of coffee. On both headboard posts the bear's elbows rested on either side of a carved heart.

"Young lady," the older woman said, slinging her arm through the air in front of Ciara. "You see a haint, dear?"

Ciara shook her head and blinked. "Nope. A bear. A bear on a bed that my grandpa swears united him and my grandma in a lifetime of love."

"A bear on a bed?" the old man laughed. "Now that could unite even people who don't like each other. Make me go running right into this lady's arms." Chuckling, he nudged toward the woman who was offering him her cheek.

Ciara snagged her cup from the counter. "Just a carved bear, but part of a magic bed according to Grandpa," she said stepping toward the door.

The barista tap danced his fingers through the air as if playing a piano. "Maybe our bear will manifest some mojo our way for the holiday."

The chime above the door tinkled as Ciara left.

Days later, Tim called Ciara from the repair shop and asked her to stop by to see if the mended bed met her standards.

After work, Ciara trotted through the front door of the shop and stopped abruptly as if she'd run into a glass wall.

The sign propped up on the bed was huge. "New Arrival, Bear Hug," it read, but the bear was what she couldn't tear her eyes from—the heart, the bear tucked in the middle with arms swaddling either side. It was her grandfather's trademark design for sure. The only difference was the engraved scarf swaying loosely around the bear's neck.

"Can I help you, Miss?" a man said, stepping to her side.

Without moving her gaze, she pointed toward the etched logo. "Who did this?"

"I like to buy local, but this is such a unique piece. It is a West Virginia-based company, so I felt good about taking it in," the skinny man said. "And the scarf! What an added touch." He feigned flipping a scarf around his neck.

"It's a trademark infringement. It has to be," Ciara said, turning and popping her hand onto her hip. "This is my grandfather's logo. It's on the bed I brought in for repair. Except the scarf."

"Oh, so you are Ciara?" the man remarked, extending his hand. "I'm Tim, the owner. I noticed the similarities to your headboard, of course. Wondered how you had an antique piece with the same engraving as this new one. I even verified the paperwork trail which led back to the Asian-based subsidiary that originally manufactured the pieces, but it's all legit. The Bear Hug Ltd. Co. maintains authentic ownership."

Ciara twisted her hair around her finger. "Asia, you say? Who is the owner of this Bear Hug?"

"I will check for you tomorrow. I have to head out to a delivery now," Tim said, directing her toward a side room where her headboard was stacked inside a storage bin. "Meanwhile, look this over and see if you can tell where it was glued." Tim puffed up his chest and rubbed his hands together like he was going to start a fire.

"Amazing," Ciara said, ogling the craftmanship and running her hands along the surface. "Smooth. You are as gifted as Matt said. I will have him pick it up this afternoon if you will be back."

"Yep," Tim nodded. "I'll be here from five 'til six o'clock."

The kitchen counter at Ciara's had been converted into an art studio. Flour and cookies dusted the far end with ribbon and netting on the other. Ciara and her friend, Marcia, were sprinkling pinecones with glitter when a horn honked out front.

Ciara pushed her bangs from her eyes with the back of her hand, grabbed a dry dishcloth and reached the door just as Matt was about to knock with his knee.

He staggered under the weight of the headboard while maneuvering through the door, then headed toward the bedroom.

"Whoa, bubba!" she said, motioning him to the basement door. "Down here."

Matt continued to her bedroom. "Baby sis, this is one time in your life you are going to listen to me," he said. Eyeing Marcia in the hall behind Ciara he added, "And Marcia, you'll hear this anyway so you might as well join in now."

Ciara opened her mouth to protest, but Matt was already rattling on about Grandma's wishes and his promise to her to assemble the bed and garner Ciara's promise that she would sleep in it at least through the Christmas season. The end of December, to be exact. After that, she could sleep on whatever bed she wanted.

Ciara snapped the dishtowel in the air. "Fine," she said and strutted to the kitchen. "Like I am going to activate some magic portal by simply sleeping in it. Poppycock!"

Matt followed her and snatched a candy cane shaped cookie. "These edible or just decoration?" he asked.

"Just one," Ciara said, placing a handful into a plastic container adorned with reindeer motifs and lined with red tissue paper. "Cookies are for the children's hospital party. Pinecone baskets for the staff."

Marcia pulled the last batch from the oven. "We'll drop them off before the parade tomorrow evening."

Later that night, Ciara snuggled into the restored bed, picked up the pink quartz stone from her stand, rubbed it between her fingers and stared into the dark sky. Not even a hint of a star could be seen, but that didn't mean there weren't any there, she reasoned.

"Star light, star bright," she whispered. "First star I know is there, wish I may, wish I might find a love as deep as night... as brave as a bear." She tossed the stone onto the table. "Not one that runs off to another country and never returns."

The next morning Ciara smacked the buzzing alarm. She picked up her paper tablet. Sketchy handwriting, but her dream journal always was messy.

"Yes!" she exclaimed, reading it. "That's right. A mama bear motioned to me to follow her. Then was raised high on her hind legs protecting her newborn cubs. She wasn't going to let the coyote hurt her babies." Ciara closed the journal, got dressed and strolled the few blocks to town while pondering the dream.

Bears were a symbol of protection and bravery, both attributes she had to fuel since Art left, but the birth theme of the dream held her focus more than any other element of symbolism. Interesting how female bears hibernate during pregnancy then wake mid-winter to give birth.

Perhaps she too could give birth after moving from the psychedelic speed of the city—birth to inspired ideas for the article on travel she'd been wanting to write, birth of a family scenario with giggling children and purring cats... and okay, a handsome hubby as charming as his smile. This was her dream, so she might as well design it right!

She made her way along Froggy Lane to the repair shop where the sign on the door crested a dark interior. "Closed for Christmas Parade."

She sighed. She would have to wait to find out who was responsible for reproducing her grandfather's furniture and pawning it off as their own.

Ciara called Marcia and they met up at the Latte Lounge before heading to the children's hospital, arms laden with cookies. They passed out the treats, each one given with a smile, and headed to the town square. Music bounced across the decorative crowd from the lamppost speakers, "It's the most wonderful time of the year..." as the gingerbread float and firetrucks passed by, baton twirlers and elves with conical hats dancing in between.

"Hot chocolate is calling," Marcia said as Matt waved from atop a float with a pine tree so large it looked as though the Grinch could crawl from underneath. Stockings hung from the branches and little lumberjacks, both boys and girls, threw candy to children scattered among the crowd.

"I'll get it," Ciara said, tugging on her crossover bag. "Feeling this way," she added and shuffled toward the center of activity. Several booths away, the crowd was thick. She diverted through the grass and was rounding the trees lit like the bioluminescent bays in Puerto Rico when she saw an outline of an animal that looked like a bear.

She grabbed the tree trunk as the animal prowled closer to the bright gazebo lights. A bear's glowing eyes called to her. *I've lost it*, she thought, forging forward. Maybe I should warn the others nearby.

She followed the bear, ducking under tree branches dripping with lights and rounded the gazebo. Scanning the crowd, she saw the grassy area where a few people lingered with strollers and drinks. No bear, but alas, the hot chocolate booth.

She ordered and turned with the two warm cups, spotting Tim at the end of the line chatting away.

Instantly he motioned her over. "Wow!" he said. "You are one lucky girl. Ciara," he said, open palm directed toward the handsome man in front of him. "Meet the man whose company constructed the bear bed that's in my shop."

If an Arctic blast had come through, she couldn't have been more frozen. Every function ceased—her brain spinning inside a cocoon of coldness, her hands no longer feeling the warmth of the hot chocolate. Her heart sure hadn't stopped beating. It pounded harder than a jackhammer busting through concrete.

"Hello," the man said, his crystal blue eyes nodding with his head.

Ciara did not move. Did not blink.

"Ciara," Tim said, adjusting his toboggan. "You look like you saw the Ghost of Christmas Past."

Marcia stepped into the group and reached for one of the cups in Ciara's stiff hands. "Thought you fell into the rabbit hole, girl."

"No ghost and no rabbits," Ciara said, shaking her head to warm it and get the gears working. "Just bears and deserters."

"You like the bed?" the man said, caressing his perfectly groomed sideburns.

"Oh," Tim said, motioning for the man to step forward in line. "This is Art Holstead, the owner of the Bear Hug company."

Marcia squealed, "Art! The Art who broke your heart?" Marcia stepped so close to Ciara the steam from their hot chocolates formed a single spout.

Tim glanced from Ciara to Art, his head bobbing. "I'm only a furniture repair guy. Repairing relationships is..." Tim looked at Marcia and shrugged. "Well that's a whole different industry."

Ciara's chin dipped into the scarf surrounding her neck and she pounded her free hand onto her hip. "No one is asking you to repair anything." Her eyes darted to Art and stuck to his like a suction cup. "An explanation for why you stole my grandfather's design would be nice."

Art folded his hands as if to pray, his lips brushing his fingertips. "I—"

"You know what? Forget it," Ciara said, nudging a wide-eyed Marcia out of line. "My attorney can handle this."

"You were right," Art said, pulling a picture from his wallet.

Ciara hesitated mid-step and waved at the blue-winged angel ringing a bell on the passing float.

Marcia grabbed Tim by the wrist and whispered in his ear as they walked off.

"About me being a workaholic," Art began. "About my company deconstructing the world bit by bit rather than creating something useful." He shuffled from one leg to the other. "I needed some time to see that for myself, but if it weren't for this man..." Art extended the picture to Ciara. "I wouldn't have had the courage to explore how I really felt about the business."

Ciara rolled her eyes. "So, you run off to find your proverbial self? This isn't a movie, Art. Life doesn't always have a happy ending."

"Exactly!" Art smiled. "A sad ending is what made me decide to contribute instead of dismantling people's lives. I facilitated a deal in Japan that closed a non-profit office and left thousands without access to a food supply. A few nights later, I'm drinking my martini and watching the news in the best penthouse in Tokyo when I see the headline. 'Tie One On For Those In Need.' Restaurants and pubs throughout the city were donating a free meal to the community kitchen for every patron wearing a scarf in support of the effort. 'The scarf,' one owner said, 'draws attention to the neck. Everyone deserves good food to swallow. The closure of the biggest non-profit in Tokyo threatens to strangle our most vulnerable of citizens.' I turned off the TV and scrolled through my phone pics. Just wanted to see your smiling face."

Ciara tucked a curl behind her ear, looked at the picture and recognized her grandfather. "How'd Grandpa help you—other than providing your furniture prototype?"

Art glanced at the young man in the booth. "One cup with marshmallows, please," he said, handing over a twenty. "And keep the change."

He turned to Ciara. "Everything you ever said to me was playing in my head," he said excitedly. "I came across a picture of you and your grandpa in the bear bed last year before Alzheimer's claimed him." Art swallowed an enormous breath. "The bear's eyes seemed to glow... and, Ciara, I swear, I heard your grandfather's voice say, 'Bear hugs help'."

Art quietly looked deep into Ciara's ocean-colored eyes. She felt like an ice cream cone in the hot summer sun, melting into him more with each word.

"I know it sounds absurd, but I recognized his voice." Art tilted his head to Heaven, a few snowflakes falling onto his cheeks. "It was as if he was encouraging me to bring his design to life again."

Her lips parted slightly; her shoulders relaxed. He was speaking from the heart and she felt it.

"Turns out your grandfather never had an official trademark on it, so I added the scarf to honor those helping prevent hunger in Japan and registered the updated design. Also, in remembrance of your grandfather, ten percent of sales is donated to Alzheimer's research."

Ciara's hands merged to form a steeple and she touched her fingertips to her lips.

Art dipped his head, peering from the corner of his eyes. "I'm sorry I hurt you. I felt you deserved someone who wasn't travelling the world, someone who could help you with the groceries and wash your car on Saturdays, take you dancing. I was a mess. I couldn't be that man, but..." Art reached for her hand. "I always wanted to be."

Ciara swallowed hard and took his hand.

Art lifted his cup. "Cheers," he said. "To the bears."

Ciara tapped her cup with his. "Bear hugs help," she said, laying her head on Art's shoulder as screams echoed through the crowd and a tiny black figure disappeared into the trees beyond the children on Santa's lap asking for what they'd like for Christmas.

Ciara already had her gift.

Tidings of Comfort and Joyce

Kimberly Kurth Gray

It was harder and harder to get arrested these days in Waverly Springs. I shifted the gear into drive, pushed my foot firmly on the gas pedal and plowed directly into the back of Chief Beau Garland's brand new Ford Expedition.

"Come on, Joyce," the chief yelled as he lumbered from his vehicle, a wide brown stain spreading across the crotch of his tan uniform pants. He stomped over to my car and rapped his huge knuckles against the glass.

"Sorry," I said as I rolled down the window, but I couldn't help smiling.

"Damn it, Joyce. Suppose that coffee'd been hot? You coulda scalded me." Beau then gestured at his crumpled SUV. "And look at my car! It took nearly five years to convince the mayor the Impala was on its last legs." He covered his face with a gloved hand and growled.

"Guess you'll have to take me in," I said unbuckling my seatbelt. "Judge Bell must be home by now spending Christmas Eve with his family, so my arraignment will have to wait until Monday." I dabbed some gloss on my lips and tossed the container in the glove compartment. They probably didn't allow beauty items in jail.

Beau leaned his arm against my car and stooped his six-foot-four body over so our noses nearly touched. It made me think of our senior prom and how he'd kissed me before opening my door. I closed my eyes and leaned toward him.

"Have you been drinking?" he asked.

Startled, I sat back in my seat. "Of course not." But then I remembered my mission. "Cooking sherry doesn't count, right?"

Beau sighed deeply. "Joyce, haven't we talked about this?"

I shifted in my seat, unwilling to meet his eyes. "Yes, but you don't..."

"Look," he said, his voice much softer now, "you can't go round getting yourself arrested every Christmas Eve just because your mother-in-law's visiting."

"Beau, if you only knew the grief that woman causes me."

"Come on, now. She comes to town for a week once a year. How terrible can that be? She just wants to spend time with her family. Old people get stuck in their ways. Can't you ignore her for seven days?"

But Carol Pine was not old. She'd been a teenager when Timothy was born and had practically grown up with him. He was more to her than a son, he was her best friend and confidant. She gave him his wake up call each morning and insisted he call her before bed every night. They took special vacations to celebrate Timothy's birthdays and had all sorts of secrets and private jokes. *"Remember dear, blood is thicker than water,"* Carol often reminded me.

"What is it really, Joyce?" Beau asked, breaking into my thoughts.

"She hates me. Has from the day I got married." I bit my lip and looked away from Beau, but his expression didn't change. "The constant nagging and criticizing of everything from my cooking to the way I wear my hair." Tears began to well up in my eyes.

Beau chuckled and the merriment of it surprised me. He'd become serious and reserved since returning to town nine years ago, far different from the fun-loving prankster I'd dated in high school.

"Joyce, go home. Park your car, have another sherry and let her do all the cooking. The week will go by quickly. Time passes like that." Beau gave a slight smile and patted the roof of my car.

I put my forehead against the steering wheel. The tears were threatening to spill down my face. I couldn't go home and face another holiday with her, or worse yet, her and Timothy together. As I pondered what to do, a car pulled up behind mine. Two doors shut and I could hear footsteps approaching.

"Officer, what seems to be the problem now?" Carol asked.

Just what I needed. It would've been one thing to deal with her on Monday after a nice quiet rest in jail, but to have to hear her berate me for seven days was too much. I'd been arrested two years ago on Christmas Eve. It was all a misunderstanding, of course. I'd inadvertently left Wagoner's Grocery with a *People* magazine tucked under my arm. When the manager approached me in the parking lot, I'd laughed. Apologizing, I handed him the magazine. It was then he told me the police had been called.

He accused me of not only shoplifting the magazine, but of stealing grapes, chocolates and strawberries. I was not a thief, I was only sampling them. "Tell it to the judge," he said. I spent Christmas Eve and most of Christmas day in a cell at the Waverly Springs Police Station. Most everybody was off for the holiday, so I spent my time watching *The Bishop's Wife* and *It's a Wonderful Life* on the portable black and white television Beau brought in for me. While we ate fried oysters from Leona's and listened to midnight mass, I began thinking how that was the nicest holiday I'd had in twenty-seven years. It was then I began to plot how to repeat it.

"Officer," Carol said again.

"It's Chief, ma'am, Chief Beau Garland."

"Chief." Carol's voice was thick with sarcasm. "I cannot imagine what Joyce has done this time, but I can assure you it was not intentional. She's quite simple minded and much too lazy to plan anything. She can barely plan a Christmas dinner let alone a criminal act."

Beau did not respond, nor did Timothy. Without lifting my head, I knew he would be standing behind his mother.

"So officer, oh, sorry, Chief, though I've no doubt you have a valid reason for holding her, let's forget about it for now. I don't want my son caused any more embarrassment or distress. Timothy, get my bag. How much will it take? Shall I write this to the station? What about you, Chief? I'm sure you wouldn't mind a little holiday bonus. Get yourself a new pair of trousers. What do you say?"

The car door was yanked open and Beau grabbed my elbow and pulled me from the seat, clunking my head against the steering wheel in the process. I gasped when he pinched handcuffs on my wrists. Timothy hung his head as if hiding behind his mother.

"Joyce Pine, I'm placing you under arrest for destruction of state property." Beau slammed the door shut with his foot and practically dragged me up the block to the station. I thought Carol or at least Timothy would follow, but as Beau escorted me inside, I saw the car pull away. Carol was driving, of course.

The building was eerily quiet with most of the employees on holiday. Only the constant ticking of the Starburst Clock could be heard. In 1950, Mayor Burt Star thought himself rather clever and gifted each public building in Waverly Springs a clock in honor of the town's bicentennial. He wasn't as remembered as he hoped and though the time was incorrect, this was the last working clock of the group.

Beau removed the cuffs and showed me into his office. He nodded at the chair beside his desk and I sat down. "What now?" he asked.

"Don't you know? We've done this the past two years. Just print me. I'm tired."

Beau opened his bottom desk drawer and retrieved a take-out menu. "Shrimp lo mein?"

That had always been my favorite. He and I would walk over to Chop Styx Louie's after our movie dates. Long ago, before he went away to college.

"You arrested me, remember?"

"Yep. You want eggrolls or spring rolls?"

"Spring rolls. So, I'm just going to sit here at your desk and eat Chinese food?"

"That's right. Unless you're anxious to get on home." Beau phoned Jimmy Wu's Asian Café, the restaurant that had replaced Chop Styx. He ordered for me the same as he'd done when we were sixteen. When he hung up the phone, he sat back into his chair and folded his hands over his stomach. Beau was no longer lean and blond, but time had still been kind to him. He wore his graying hair shorter now and the closely trimmed beard and mustache were new.

I tried to relax but more knots formed than untied in my stomach. Suddenly, I was self-conscious of my appearance. Were my bangs too short? Why had I worn this horrible green coat? It should have been thrown away two winters ago. Under it was my best dress, a pink floral cotton with ruffles down the front that poked out between the coat's buttons. It was definitely not warm enough for this season, but I wanted to look nice for my mug shot. Beau Garland hadn't even crossed my mind when I was choosing it.

"They said it'd be about forty-five minutes," Beau said and handed me a mug of black coffee. He kept his gaze steady on my face as he sat back down.

"Thanks." I could barely get the word out.

"Look, Joyce, there's something I've been wanting to say to you for a while now."

"Beau, don't. You don't need to say anything. What happened, happened. It was thirty years ago."

"Twenty-seven, and it'll be twenty-eight on March third." He scooted his chair around the desk and closer to me. "Noelle Green was just a girl. I was twenty-one, not more than a kid and not thinking of anybody but myself. I never wanted to hurt you, Joyce. I've always..."

"Come in, Chief," a voice squawked from the radio.

"What's up?" Beau replied pressing in a button.

"We got a situation down here at Wagoner's. A woman threatened the manager. She's been uncooperative. Hey, lady, knock it off." The officer's voice crackled out.

"Bring her in." Beau shut the radio off. Whatever he'd begun to say was now lost. He went over to a small table and fiddled with a can of coffee. "You know, you could always go down to Florida and spend Christmas with your own mother."

I unbuttoned my coat and pink ruffles spilled out like they were happy to escape the confines of the heavy wool. "Mom goes on a cruise every Christmas. She has a group of friends she travels with now."

Beau refilled my mug. "Going to a prom?" he asked, looking my dress over.

"No," I answered. My face grew warm and I hoped it wasn't the same shade as my dress. "It's... I mean, I was going..."

"You look nice. You always do."

I took several sips of my coffee trying to hide. I didn't know how to respond.

"What could I have said? I didn't know what to say to you." Beau's words were quiet and hesitant.

"It's my fault. It was all my fault. I shouldn't have come out there to see you. I should have given you a chance to explain." I didn't want to talk about this, now or ever. I had gone to West Virginia to surprise Beau at college, had saved every penny for the bus fare and the motel. The surprise, however, was on me. His roommate helped me to sneak into the dorm all the while knowing Beau was with someone else.

All through high school I'd worried Beau would grow tired of me. He was a football hero and I was a shy girl who spent most of her days trying to be invisible. When I saw Noelle Green strut nude from Beau's bed, all tall and tan and blonde, I knew my fears had been valid. I shuddered at the memory.

"You cold?"

"No, I'm fine. Let's not talk about this, okay?"

"Okay," he said then pressed his lips tightly together as if to hold in all he had wanted to say.

I'd caught the next bus home after finding Beau with Noelle and rushed right into a relationship with Timothy. I married him weeks later, the day after the pregnancy test read positive. Though I'd not managed to carry any of my pregnancies more than several weeks, I'd held onto the marriage.

"I thought, hoped really, that you'd come after me," I said, bringing up the subject I'd moments ago ended.

"Joyce."

"I'm sorry. Just forget it." I placed my mug on his desk.

Beau came and crouched beside me so close I could feel his breath on my cheek as he spoke. "Joyce, I was ashamed of what I had done. I should've come right home to see you instead of waiting for the semester to end. You'd gone and married Timid," Beau smiled. "I mean Timothy. It happened so fast."

It had been fast, too fast. After dating Beau for four years, I'd married Timothy in four weeks. It had been silly, stupid and rash. In trying to punish Beau, I'd spent years punishing myself instead. There was nothing I could change about it now.

The front door of the station house slammed shut. I hoped the food was here and we could eat instead of talk, but there were too many voices to be the delivery guy.

"Miss, if you would listen for one minute." It was the same voice that had come over the radio.

Beau stood and walked toward his office door.

"Do you realize who I am?" Carol's tone was close to shrieking. "This is absolutely ludicrous."

"Miss, you've been charged with assaulting a police officer."

"I barely touched you. Timothy, get my bag. I'm sure this all can easily be rectified. How much does an assault ticket cost?"

"Miss, you've been arrested. Please step this way."

Beau put his finger to his lips and silently slid the door closed. He picked his hat up from the desk along with his keys. "Come with me," he whispered and held out his hand.

I didn't hesitate to grab hold. We ran out the back door into the night, the falling snow covering our tracks.

THE BRIDGE ON THE RIVER OBI–WAN

Ramona DeFelice Long

It is Christmas Eve, and I am done. Done with shopping, done with decorating, done with watching my husband head out for the evening shift *again*, leaving me with two antsy boys *again*, on the eve of a holiday.

By the time he leaves, I am so done with it all that I sit down to watch television—during the day. I never watch TV during the day, particularly this one, when I am normally baking or wrapping gifts or searching for dress pants that fit my long-legged sons, or doing something befitting the frantic holiday season. This year, though, I planned ahead, and so got it all done in advance. Only took a decade to smarten up.

I should feel good, self-satisfied, accomplished instead of grinding about being alone. Later, the boys and I will open one Christmas Eve gift, then we'll have party foods and watch a Christmas movie we've seen a hundred times before. They'll beg to open one more gift. Or maybe all of them. That's the plan.

I already know the reality: I will count the minutes until their dad comes home. I will give in twice and let them open three gifts instead of one. I will stay up too late and be grumpy and groggy when they wake at the crack of dawn. I will get annoyed at my husband when he puts on a happy holiday face while all I want to do is mainline coffee. Because Christmas makes me *done*.

But that's tomorrow. Today, to my surprise, I find a good movie to watch, a classic I've seen as many times as the holiday film we'll watch tonight, but it's been a long time. I settle in. Maybe the day can turn around after all.

I'm not alone for long. My eleven-year-old son— banished not long ago to "find something to do, for God's sake!"—meekly enters the family room. He looks momentarily stunned by my inactivity.

"Hi, Mom. What are you watching?"

He smiles, big and fake, which makes my mom antenna rise. He only smiles like that when he wants something. I assume it's the television.

"I am watching," I announce, "one of the best films ever made." I don't mention that it is one of my personal favorites. I don't want him to exit on the run.

He looks at the television. "Oh, yeah? What's it rated?"

Not "What's it called?" or "What's it about?" or "Who's in it?" or "Why is it one of the best movies ever made?" The rating is all he cares about. He's hoping I'll say that it's rated R because even though *all of his friends* get to watch R-rated films, he is not allowed.

"It's not rated," I answer, squelching my desire to gloat because I am, after all, a grown-up. "It was made before the movie ratings started."

"Oh," is all he can say. He doesn't move. He also doesn't ask for the TV. Not yet. Because he is my child, I know that he is contemplating his next move. He's thinking that it's the day before a major holiday and surely I'll have some urgent chore to do soon, so if he just waits it out, he can avoid a "the TV belongs to all of us" discussion.

I don't want to deliver that talk again, either. I'm pleased to have dodged another skirmish in the battle of the R, but I really do want to see this movie. After a few silent moments, he launches into Plan B, pretending to be interested in something Mom likes.

"What's it called?"

"*The Bridge on the River Kwai.* It's a World War II movie."

"Oh, yeah?"

He knows about World War II. He's studied Pearl Harbor and Hitler and the atomic bomb in school. We've visited the Holocaust Museum. He knows about D-Day, too. Some kids at school, kids with *nice* moms, have seen *Saving Private Ryan.*

He looks at the screen. A British medic is lecturing fellow prisoners on why it would be foolhardy to try to escape from their Japanese captors. The scene is in a makeshift hospital in the jungle. Everyone is sweaty but, oddly, there is no blood.

"Are you sure this is a war movie? 'Cause I don't see any guns."

"It's a war movie."

"With no guns?"

"They're POWs. They're in a prison camp in the middle of the jungle."

Prisoners in a jungle prison camp. This has possibilities.

"Tell me about it," he commands and flops down beside me.

I hesitate. He has entered the pre-adolescent, adversarial stage, and I'm his primary opponent. Lately, everything I utter—from homework instructions to fashion advice—results in impatient sighs or "M-O-M" accompanied by an eye-rolling death stare. Anything I say can and will be used against me, and I assume that includes film critiques.

Nevertheless, it's been a while since he's deigned to sit beside me, so I try to explain. It's not a simple movie. It's set in Burma. It is based on true events, about captured British soldiers forced to build a railway bridge in the middle of the jungle. It focuses on the British and the Japanese, with only one American in camp and not a single Nazi in sight.

Luckily, in the middle of my synopsis, armed guards appear, also sweating, and so my son accepts that it is indeed a war movie.

"*What* are they talking about? What's the big deal about the bridge?"

I forge in. The British prisoners don't want to build a bridge that will help the enemy's war effort, so they are faking sickness to get out of doing the work. For my son, this concept needs no further explanation.

"Why don't they just escape?"

I repeat what the medic said about it being virtual suicide to venture into the dry, barren area beyond the camp. I also tell him that, just before he walked in, three prisoners found outside the perimeter of the work area were lined up and shot.

"What's happening now?"

The two enemy colonels, the British Nicholson and Japanese Saito, have reached an impasse about the bridge work. To Saito's frustration, Nicholson stands firm by the rules of the Geneva Convention that officers cannot be forced to perform manual labor.

"Hey! That's not fair," Son says. It's his daily mantra: *Why can't I XYZ? My friend so-and-so gets to XYZ.*

Sometimes I want to line up so-and-so's parents and... well, I'm a pacifist, so I can't. "How come only the regular guys have to work?"

"Officers are supposed to lead and guide, in battle and when they are captured. They're responsible for supervising their men. It's just like how it's my responsibility to supervise you to make your bed and do your laundry and pack your lunch, but you still have to do it yourself."

He gives me a look of supreme disappointment. He's honored me with his presence, he's listened to me go on about an un-rated movie, and I reward him with a *lecture?* He scoots forward, ready to leave.

And then they stick Colonel Nicholson in the tin oven out in the blazing sunshine.

"What's that thing?"

This time, I avoid making any analogies between this colonel baking all day in a small tin room and my son using the Constitution as a reason not to wear a belt with his school uniform. I explain that Nicholson is refusing to break the tenets of the Geneva Convention, so the Japanese are putting him in this hot box with no food or water as punishment.

Son watches and is torn. He's hostile toward Nicholson over the work controversy, but admires the man's stamina in the oven. On the other hand, the Japanese colonel is clearly the enemy, but it still seems like the British officers are getting away with a fast one. Who do you root for in a case like this?

I remain silent while he watches. Nicholson is dragged out, parched and starving, and Saito tempts him with a steak. My son likes steak. He gets it that they're trying to psyche each other out. I venture an opinion.

"They're not really arguing about the bridge," I say. "They're arguing about honor."

He looks at me. "Huh?"

"Saito believes that any type of surrender is dishonorable, but the British don't agree. They may have been defeated in that one battle, but they should still be treated like soldiers."

I don't say that this is what I mean about how losing a basketball game doesn't make you a loser or how what you do when you're out in the world shows how you feel about yourself. I don't say Colonel Nicholson may be elitist and old-fashioned, but he's got a truckload of self-esteem.

"Well," my son says, "I'd still try to escape."

I tell him that Nicholson forbade attempts at escape. I remind him that the three guys who tried were shot. My son finally agrees that escaping is not a good idea, and then William Holden, the American, escapes.

"You said they couldn't escape!"

"*I* didn't say they couldn't escape. The British officers said it."

"It's because he's American," Son decides. "Those British dudes just aren't tough enough."

I am tempted to point out that the business of the oven says plenty about the toughness of British dudes, but instead speak his language. "Whatever."

"I still don't get it. What does this have to do with the bridge?"

We've been over that, I want to say, but some lessons bear repeating. "Nicholson believes in following rules, no matter what. Saito has been ordered to get the bridge built, no matter what. They're having a war of wills."

"So, who's right?"

How do I answer? We have battles like this. Not over a bridge or honor, but over R-rated movies and what isn't fair and what friends get to do but he doesn't. The intellectual part of me accepts that such arguments are a natural and necessary part of his growing up process. And even when I win a round, it never feels much like a victory, but how do you surrender what's best for your child?

I understand Nicholson's resolve. My son may bicker over fairness and boundaries, but I think, I *hope,* he knows that I would go into an oven for him. So I pull a parent's trick and ask who *he* thinks is right.

He watches the screen. He doesn't know yet. And then a look comes over his face. He leans forward, staring hard at Nicholson.

"I know him," he says slowly. "That voice...That's Obi-Wan! You didn't tell me Obi-Wan was in this movie!"

I have no answer. When I think of Alec Guinness, it's Colonel Nicholson I recall, not the *Star Wars* guy.

So much for serious contemplation of fairness and honor. Neither the British Empire nor a Japanese dynasty can surpass the credibility of a Jedi knight.

We watch together. Nicholson lectures his men on the value of hard work. He states his proper bridge concept, and I run with it. He may be a master with a light saber, but I have enough parenting experience to recognize a life lesson when it smacks me in the face.

"You get what the colonel, I mean, Obi-Wan is saying?"

I give the speech about working to your ability and being proud of your efforts whether you are a prisoner or an officer or a kid. And out of respect for Jedis everywhere, my son listens.

But when we reach the climax, I realize this movie probably *should* be rated R. Not for violence or language or sex, but for that confusing gray area called mature themes.

The proper bridge is built, but destroyed; the train crashes, but the American hero dies. Saito is humiliated but meets his deadline, and Nicholson blows up the bridge—and himself—after realizing his terrible mistake.

Madness, the wise doctor calls it.

It's madness, all right, but it would be madder still not to try to explain this to a child who won't be under my command for much longer. Who, when I give in about opening more gifts, will squeal with excitement, who will hug me at bedtime, who will tell me the party foods are his favorites, who will pretend to be asleep when his father comes home at midnight, just in time to put out milk and cookies for Santa Claus.

It's time to get the ham in the oven, but my son stays on the sofa while the camera pans over the final shots, of dead bodies and the destroyed bridge. I stay on the sofa, too. The ham can wait. I want to hear my son's movie review.

Marching music begins and the credits roll.

My son shakes his head. "Man," he says, "he was a lot easier to understand when he was Obi-Wan."

On this, we agree.

REMINISCING ON THE NOSTALGIA
OF HAPPIER TIMES

Amy Morley

Seventeen years ago, our meeting
at the South Street Seaport
gave me faith, hope, longing
to believe in not only you, but in myself too.

Parade ended hours earlier,
sight-seeing in the city that
defines Christmas
I look up to see the unseeable guest of honor
walking by the pier.

Your crimson coat with pearl cuffs,
  boots as black as coal for the naughty ones looked so
    real...

  Hearing the bells on your belt jingle in sweet melody
singing the songs only children can hear...

  How is it possible to still believe in a mythical being
    that cannot be seen?

Virginia wondered, as did Van Allsburg.
Now here I am, aged fifteen, selected as one of the
 chosen

to go back
to a happier time,
to rejoice in miracles,

to believe in magic.

Today I hold on to this memory,
though it feels like yesterday
when innocence was born.

I still believe in you,
while grasping my childhood, and
reminiscing on the nostalgia of happier times,
never doubting your existence.

  Perhaps it was only a dream, a child-like memory
    invented, or
  simply the magic of the season
  during a magical time
  with the magic of words exchanged when you finally
    spoke:
"I'll believe in you if you keep believing in me,"
to which I whispered my reply,
"I believe."

And so I believe I was one of the few
in this world,
in this lifetime,
graced with your magic a childhood ago
holding on to the hope
to believe another miracle.

CHRISTMAS PEARL

Demi Stevens

Alicia sat on the guestroom floor amidst a pile of wrapping paper and ribbons, waging battle with the last of the presents. She saw it as one of many non-paid contributions she made to her husband's career. There were no toys to assemble, or dolls or trucks. Instead she methodically stacked embossed books, monogrammed pens and gift cards to "The Club."

Tom's constituency always came first, and by *constituency* she meant his campaign contributors. He would never publicly declare the real reason he'd voted against labor unions was that Southwood Club's elite were livid about the new association of PGA caddies who commanded a percentage of the golfer's winnings, above and beyond their hefty salary. Never mind that his club paid its loopers only a pittance.

She absentmindedly fingered the solitary pearl suspended from a length of yarn around her neck. Usually it was hidden behind neck-gripping sweaters or buried in the cleavage of her specialty bra, but today she could just be herself in a ragged Georgia State sweatshirt. Blessedly it was a day without charity dinners or art galas or the mind-numbing campaign stumping that awaited next spring.

With the gift-wrapping behind her, Alicia settled on their sunny Georgia patio with a virgin mimosa. These days it seemed every part of her body betrayed her. A bladder infection was the latest in a parade of chemo side-effects. Worse was the cloudy memory following surgery. Mere days before Christmas, she still couldn't raise the energy to pull out the decorations.

Instead, she mindlessly caressed the dangling pearl.

In a fit of self-disgust she pushed up from the white wicker and made her way through a set of French doors which opened directly into the master suite. From there she entered the walk-in closet, arranged meticulously by season and style. Selecting a modest golf top and pants, topped by a zippered running jacket, she donned pristine white socks and sneakers, then set out to Southwood's snakepit with her clubs already packed in the Mercedes.

Alicia had to work hard to smile at the valet. In truth, she preferred to park her own car, but Tom had lectured her on the value of appearances and good tipping.

"Getting in a few holes this afternoon, Mrs. M?" the young man asked while she dug through her designer bag for a fiver, then opted for a ten.

"Perhaps," Alicia answered. "Can you see if Johnny would carry out my clubs?" She looked down to the ground as she said the other man's nickname.

"Right away, *ma'am*."

She could feel the attendant bristle after she hadn't spoken to him by first name as well. Trying not to slight the boy, she reached into her foggy brain. "I'd really appreciate it, *Patrick*."

His smile was all the reward she needed, though he seemed more enthusiastic about the cash.

Alicia straightened her spine and walked under the canopied entrance.

An older man was just leaving, but held the door for her. "Why hello, Alicia, dear. I must say you're looking lovely today. Will your busy husband be joining you for a quick round?"

Again she racked her brain for a name. "Oh... Mr. Jacobs," she said with a sigh. "Tom could never sneak away in the middle of the day." But perhaps *someone* could.

Alicia watched as Johnny lovingly cleaned and polished the driver before replacing it in the bag with her other clubs.

"You know you could store these here in your member's locker..." he said, then hefted the bag for their walk to the green.

She admired the muscles bulging under his tight cotton shirt, before forcing herself to meet his gaze. "But then I'd miss out on your extra... attentions." Suddenly bashful, she turned to contemplate the immaculately cut grass.

Johnny had been her husband's caddie for fifteen years, starting as a college summer job the year Tom took office. When her husband finally talked her into learning to play—so she could schmooze his contributors' wives—he'd wanted to make sure she would be accompanied by someone who wouldn't spread gossip.

"Jonathan is the soul of discretion," Tom had assured.

That was an understatement. Alicia remembered how Johnny had thoughtfully guided her away from rookie mistakes during those painful first foursomes. And not just the golf, but also knowing how to respond to the catty chatter of the other women. Johnny's whispered reassurances had been all that kept her going after the mastectomy.

"Your game is really improving," he said today. "Too bad Mrs. Adams stood you up. The whole of Southwood would have heard about this birdie you're about to make."

Alicia's smile faded. If Tom got wind of the lie she'd told at the desk to cover up why she was golfing solo, it would take a lot of explaining. "I'm sure Mrs. Adams has more important gossip to spread."

"Well," Johnny's voice purred. "I'm grateful she's not here. My afternoon just got a whole lot brighter."

This brought back her smile. "Mine, too," she whispered demurely.

He set the bag down and pulled out a mallet putter. Alicia mused that his grip upon it was delicate yet firm. Apparently not satisfied with how it had been stored, he took a chamois cloth from his pocket and began buffing the club's handle.

"You've been cheating on me," he said.

Alicia watched each measured stroke of his hand. "You were the one who was too busy with Mr. Jacob's wife last time I came. I was forced to endure the whole course with only Patrick for..." she searched for the right word then added, "...*help*. I hope he parks cars better than he caddies."

Her fingers drifted to the solitary pearl she'd released from its hiding place.

Johnny's eyes followed her movement, sending a warmth to her core. He'd never once stopped admiring her femininity after the surgery. Not like her husband.

Alicia blushed and tucked the jewel back under her collar, then took the proffered putter. She hadn't worn the prosthetic bra today. It itched like crazy, and she'd discovered that without it, her swing improved dramatically.

Lining up to the hole, she could feel the heat of Johnny's appraising stare. "That's it, Mrs. Monroe. Just a little tap and you'll have it."

Her desire for sinking the putt was not nearly as strong as the one she now barely kept in check. "Johnny, I thought we agreed you'd call me by my first name. Don't we know each other pretty well by now?"

"Not as well as I'd like to know you... *Alicia*." His throaty tone sent a tingle through her.

At last. There it was in the open—the confirmation she'd been waiting for.

Alicia turned to go to him, but caught sight of two gentlemen already lining up at the tee behind her. Maybe with another lucky drive she could outpace them on the next hole and steal a private moment for what she was sure would be a mind-blowing kiss.

"So you'd like that?" she asked before turning back to the hole. "Just a little tap?" she added with a playful wiggle.

It was all she could manage to sink the ball while her imagination ran rampant. The eleventh hole skirted a freshwater pond ahead, filled with towering irises and sweetflag grass that would shield them from prying eyes.

Johnny's touch lingered overlong as he passed the driver. In those early days, it had been par for the course to land her ball in the water hazard, but she'd have to concentrate today if she wanted to slice the swing on purpose.

Again she could feel Johnny's appraising eyes settle on her backside. The unseasonal heat was nothing compared to the warmth she now felt coursing through her body. Its tingle turned painful when she remembered her current plague of a bladder infection. Today would not be a good day for indulging all her lusts, but it would be enough just to be touched again. Caressed. Unlike the cold distance that was all Tom seemed able to muster since her surgery.

Johnny cleared his throat. "You're lined up a little funny there."

She didn't pause a moment longer. With the backswing of a newbie, she let loose on the ball and watched it sail in a tragic arc, dropping with a plop in the center of her target.

"If I didn't know better," he said with a mischievous grin, "I'd have thought you planned that."

Johnny's touch as he retrieved the club shot sparks across her gloved fingers.

"I... I..." she stammered. But the sound of a golf cart grinding into reverse brought her back to reality. The fuzziness in her brain lifted like a cloud. There would never be privacy at Southwood, or any wood for that matter. Tom would find out his faithful caddie was no more trustworthy than his wife. It would ruin his career, but also their marriage. Alicia had no doubt which one he'd regret losing more.

Alicia carefully lit the pillar candles along the mantle and selected a popular holiday playlist. Their annual Christmas Eve guests would arrive any minute, so next she walked through to check the propane heaters around the outdoor seating area. It created a perfect warmth to the fifty-degree evening.

She'd felt guilty about asking the housekeeper to decorate the tree that morning, and even worse that she hadn't remembered to invite sweet Mr. Jacobs and his wife. Hopefully Tom could smooth over any misunderstanding.

Without worrying that her dress might wrinkle, she plopped down on a chaise and reached instinctively to feel the solitary pearl beneath her neckline. It was the one memento she'd kept of the days long before her husband became a politician. Before either of them had graduated, when he'd lavished her with attention. Before the miscarriages. Before the surgery. Before the cold front.

Her guilty conscience flashed images of what might have occurred at the club a few days earlier. Instead she'd fled like an insecure schoolgirl, claiming a sudden headache.

Ah, she mused, *Johnny was probably just flirting to get a bigger tip.*

The doorbell rang and an attendant ushered in Mr. Jacobs. *Tom must have reminded him!* Alicia rushed through to the living room just in time to greet him as her husband waltzed in, dapper in a suit and tie.

"Bill, you old shark," Tom said. "I owe you a drink since you rousted me so thoroughly on the course this week."

Alicia felt her pulse quicken. Had Tom been at the club that day? Was that why Mr. Jacobs assumed she'd been meeting him?

"In that case, I'll take a bourbon, neat," Mr. Jacobs replied.

"And where's the lovely Missus?" Tom asked, looking around the room. "You didn't make her park the car, did you?"

The color drained from the older man's face but he simply replied, "She couldn't make it."

Alicia felt a need to rescue her guest, so she wrapped a hand around his elbow and guided him to a chair in the next room while Tom went to pour drinks. Her husband really did look handsome that evening.

"You're a sweetheart of a gal, Alicia. You know that, right?" Mr. Jacobs apparently hadn't recovered from his earlier upset.

"And you're a charmer, Bill," she answered and patted his hand. Probably he and the other older guests had nowhere else to go on Christmas Eve, abandoned by their offspring for ski trips and raucous parties. Maybe Tom's party for contributors was a good thing after all.

"That husband of yours talks about you all the time."

Never took you for a liar. "Is that so? And what does he say?" Alicia baited.

But the doorbell rang before he could answer, and then Tom appeared laden with a drinks tray. She excused herself to welcome the next guests.

Mrs. Adams bustled in wearing a mink better suited for Canadian weather. *"Dah-ling,"* she oozed as she extended the coat to one side as if waiting for a butler.

Alicia side-stepped and scooped it in both hands to keep the hem from dragging. Maybe Tom had been forced to invite the woman for some reason. He knew she hated the chinwaggers. "So glad you could make it, Diane."

"I wouldn't have missed the show for anything!" Mrs. Adams, a not-so recent widow, practically beamed. "Or didn't you hear about Betty Jacobs' little *involvement* at the club? It's all anyone can talk about."

Honestly, you just got here. "I'm afraid that's out of the question. Bill is in the next room with Tom. The men got the jump on us."

"Oh darling, it's that young buck Jonathan who got the jump on Betty, actually. The valet caught them *in flagrante* on the back nine."

"What?" Alicia's mouth went dry. Betty Jacobs was twice Johnny's age. Surely Mrs. Adams was just serving up a holiday helping of exaggeration.

"Day before yesterday. I can't believe you didn't know. I mean..." the widow was practically salivating as she added, "...he caddies for you, right?"

"I... um..." Alicia's imagination delivered a picture of what might've happened just beyond that tall grass on the eleventh hole. "Honestly, I had no idea," she choked out.

"If you ask me," Mrs. Adams said unbidden, "that boy needs to keep his own club in check."

Just after midnight, the last of the guests departed. It had taken every ounce of Alicia's strength to maintain her smile and struggle with people's names and children and pets... all the things a good politician's wife was supposed to be able to do.

Tom had stayed remarkably close to her all evening. He'd even complimented her dress, and at one point, looked at her in that boyish way and timidly brushed a hand across her cheek while his eyes grazed her neckline.

She now collected stemware from the patio. As Alicia headed to the kitchen, she passed the chair where Bill Jacobs had sat only briefly. It hadn't taken long for Mrs. Adams' venom to reach its intended target.

Though it pained her to admit, Alicia actually felt more sorry for Betty. It was all too easy to imagine how the older woman must've fallen for Johnny's good looks and attentive nature. Alicia hadn't been able to eat after hearing the news, as if the catered buffet held only guilt and reprobation.

"Sweetheart," she heard Tom's voice call from the living room. "Leave those glasses for tomorrow and come in here."

Refusing to be ordered around, she carried the stemware to the sink before returning. Just because he'd sent the caterers home early didn't mean there wasn't work to be done.

To her surprise, he'd stripped off his suit jacket. The elegant tie dangled around his open shirt collar, and for a moment, she remembered how Tom had looked back in his college debate team days.

He stepped to her side, and without checking her impulse, Alicia allowed his arm to encircle her waist and draw her close. She felt his breath on her ear, and a split second later the scrape of his long leg against her hip.

"Mmm... I've missed you," he said.

His voice was different now. No longer the people-pleasing center of attention. Just Tom. Her smart, sexy partner.

"I..." she began, but his lips stopped her words. Alicia's knees went weak as the taste of his kiss was also *just Tom*. She marveled that he'd made it through the party without the bourbon his cronies so loved.

"Here," he motioned to the sofa. "Sit with me." Then he pulled her gently down beside him.

From an end table he plucked up a narrow box covered in silver paper and a thin ribbon. It wasn't one she remembered wrapping.

"Open it, sweetheart." His eyes sparkled as he pushed it into her hands.

Alicia couldn't help smiling. In the old days they had always exchanged gifts on Christmas Eve. But for the better part of two decades they'd collapsed into bed when the last donors left the party, then half-heartedly swapped holiday cards the next morning over coffee.

"But I didn't get you..." Alicia was suddenly embarrassed. How could she have known he would get her a gift this year?

"Honey, you've been through so much," Tom said. "It's reminded me..."

Alicia's cheeks colored. Of course he'd bring up the surgery. He was only doing this because he felt sorry for her.

"It reminded me," he repeated, "of how strong and beautiful you are." His hand brushed her cheek for the second time that evening.

What?

She now felt his hand drop to the high neckline of her dress and fumble under the edge. Instinctively she reached to stop him. But it was too late.

Clutching the length of yarn, he tugged until the pearl popped above the fabric, then let it dangle loose again.

Another wave of embarrassment cascaded over Alicia.

"Sweetheart, it means the world to me that after all these years, you've kept this little pearl. When I first noticed you wearing it after the surgery, I knew you'd be okay if I just gave you enough time and space. Do you remember?"

Remember?

Alicia remembered the pain of the drains, the veil of the drugs, and the endless tears she cried when she saw the scars. But she also remembered Tom taking business calls by her bedside and sleeping in a chair in her hospital room with his laptop and cell phone constantly dinging. At least he'd stayed, even if he couldn't pry himself away from politics.

"You were so beautiful that night after the dance when we drove to the shore. I can still see you now with your pants legs rolled up, barefoot, trooping through the sand."

Alicia struggled to recall the college years. Tom had found an oyster bed and delicately probed a handful of them before retrieving the gray natural pearl. He'd later drilled the hole for her and she'd strung it on a piece of yarn because they were saving all their money to get married and rent a place together after graduation.

Her hands trembled now around the metallic wrapping paper. She eased the ribbon off, and held her breath as her manicured fingertips pried open the tape and then lifted the box lid to reveal a slender silver chain with an ornate clasp.

"When I gave you that pearl," Tom said, "you told me it had been born out of the oyster's pain. But I think that's what makes it more beautiful. Just like you."

Tears welled in Alicia's eyes, and for the first time in years she felt her husband's love washing over her like the waves on that long-ago shore.

"Sometimes it takes pain to remind us," he said. "Everything can heal... if we just give it enough time."

Then Tom gently untied the yarn and threaded the pearl onto its new necklace. He motioned for her to pivot on the couch. She did so and lifted her hair as his graceful hands hooked the clasp. A moment later she felt those same warm hands travel down the slope of her shoulders.

"I love you, sweetheart..." he whispered. "My Christmas pearl."

ONCE UPON A LIFE WELL SPENT

Hilary Hauck

M ost candles don't expect a long existence, though a satisfying one shouldn't be beyond hope. Providing people with a little light against the darkness, being useful, that's what we're made for. But I'd long ago given up any such hope.

It's hard to say when my life began. The days just strummed by. People—women mostly—in a steady stream handing over coins and taking us wherever it was they took us. The candle man making rows and rows and rows of us. The bright moments of those days when his wife opened the kitchen door releasing wafts of her culinary endeavors. Cinnamon, my firm favorite.

I never expected to leave my shelf in the darkest, dustiest back corner. I leaned to the right, my shelf-fellows similarly slanted, or cracked, or flawed. A fellowship of discards. We couldn't even slip into the bundles of candles the man packaged for large orders. I used to dream of being sent out with as many others as possible. The reason for this is somewhat embarrassing, not something you'd expect of a candle, but I confess, I am rather afraid of the dark.

Yes, I'd resigned myself all right. But everything changed one morning when the snow pelted sideways outside and the candle man began pulling candles from my shelf. Could it be we cracked and crooked candles might finally hope for a home?

He took a fellow very close to me. I should have realized something was awry because there was no customer to drop a coin on the desk, but hope reigns eternal.

Well, in this case hope was dashed quickly. Instead of rolling the fellow in a sheet of thin paper, the candle man put him back in the melting pot. The familiar smell of tallow filled the air. We couldn't all be beeswax. I suppose I should have been grateful just to exist, but the stench choked me.

The candle man, in his normal steady manner, took something from a tin with a scoop he'd fashioned from paper. He emptied the contents into the melting pot. Whatever it was made an almighty bang and hot wax shot everywhere—the ceiling, the floor, the candle man.

His wife rushed in with a gust of beef stew and ushered him out of the room, leaving us to contemplate the spattered innards of what had so recently been our shelf-mate.

A tragedy. All that time waiting and he'd never find out what it felt like to be lit.

The candle man returned much later with a bandage on his hand, one on his chin. He scraped up the innards and came back to our shelf. This time I felt no excitement about the prospect of finding a home, just dread. The same fate happened to this next fella. It had to be whatever the candle man was pouring through the scoop. Nobody had ever exploded before. Nobody had had anything poured in them from a tin.

It was some days later when the candle man returned to our shelf of outcasts. His hand stretched across and I almost willed it to take another, but who was I to wish that fate on anyone else? Alas, his fingers curled around me. Whatever the reason he had taken it upon himself to explode us, we were his creations, so we did his will.

He dropped me headfirst into the melting pot. My last and final thought was that if today was baking day, his wife would open the door to the aroma of cinnamon and I'd not be there to smell it.

It was most unexpected when I felt his hand around me once more. Unexpected, and an immense relief because it meant that if his hand was around my middle, I wasn't splattered. There was hope yet.

I was changed. No doubt about that. I must say I felt like a candle. My outsides solid, yet my insides tickled. It felt like I had grit throughout. Now what holy heck was this? Elongated, too. My form thinner this time, if I wasn't mistaken. Would I even be able to stand up this tall? As I pondered my new form, I noticed something quite miraculous. The smell of the bakery was closer than ever before. So close, it actually seemed to be inside of me. I smelled of cake! Cinnamon sweet! Now if the grit on my insides was making that smell, I'd put up with it, holy heck or not.

Instead of going back on the discard shelf, the candle man put me on another shelf, the one nearest the beeswax.

I tried to get a glimpse of my fellow discards because I wanted to reassure the others I was okay.

I'd barely had time to set when the candle man pulled me back off again. Gracious, please let this not be a mistake. I didn't want to go back to tallow. I did not want to explode. But he didn't put me back to tallow. He wrapped a strip of burlap around my middle, coarse and a little itchy, and stuck a sprig of holly inside it. Prickly where the holly leaf points pressed up against me, yet uncomfortable as I was, I smelled of cinnamon. I was not being scraped from the candle man's chin and the floor.

I could put up with this.

I stood proudly on the shelf, pleased with my outfit, and with the fact that I could, tall as I was, still stand upright. Not quite with the beeswax, but I'd made it to a limelight of sorts.

Whether it was my wrapping or my scent, I didn't stay long in the shop. I barely got a glimpse of the lady who dropped a single coin on the table for me, except I did notice she wore a shabby shawl, which, from inside my fine tissue paper wrapping—green to match the holly sprig—I could tell smelled of age. It didn't appear that anyone else got wrapped with me, a fact confirmed when I arrived at my new house, tiny as it was.

A pan hung over the fire in the hearth, turnip stew if I had to guess. A far lesser enticement than the meaty stews the candle man's wife made. Not another candle in sight. It did worry me. It worried me greatly, though reminding myself that I'd not been splattered helped.

Set in pride of place in the middle on the dining room table, I watched the family eat. Mother, father, a girl and a boy. Each spooned their food slowly, without enthusiasm though with a degree of reverence. I got the sense that food might be scarce. Heat, too. The fire petered; if they didn't put wood on soon it'd go out.

By the time they had cleared away, I had begun to itch like crazy on the outside, sore as a tack in the foot on the inside. I yearned for them to light me just to put me out of my misery.

The girl brought a plate with a single red candy on it, the boy a full glass of water. They left them right next to me. Then the two children hung stockings on the mantle. To dry, one would presume.

Next, to my delight and sorrow, the mother picked me up and carried me to the hearth. This was it. This was what I'd been created for. The beginning of my end. She held me gently against a lick of flame in the fireplace. My wick pinched as it lit.

Oh, the marvel! Cinnamon perfumed the room.

I glowed proudly. A little shy at first at being the center of attention, then I warmed to my role and looked at my family to see their delight at my flame. Only they weren't delighted. They weren't even looking at me. They were readying for bed.

That was it? I wasn't even going to be seen? I would glow and extinguish to an empty room? I know, I know, we were created for one task and one task only, and how people decided that task would be done was their prerogative, but this was certainly not the way I'd ever imagined I'd snuff out. Yet to bed they went.

Pitch night outside, the fire faded, mere embers now. The night encroached and I, the only defense against it. A solitary end while my family slept.

What else would one do but reflect back on moments of existence? And that's exactly what I was doing when I heard a rustling and bumping from the fireplace.

Lords alive, a portly man in a bright red suit appeared feet first, then swung from the fireplace. I'd never seen anyone come into a house that way. And I'd never seen a burglary, if that was what was happening.

You must understand my frustration at being simply a narrator and not a participant in the world around me. If I'd had a stinking ion of an ability to shout, I would have yelled at him and yelled for my new family, because I counted them as such even if they'd opted not to watch as I burned, all alone in the dark. If I'd been able to move, I would have clobbered this red-suited fiend over the head and lit his big black boots on fire.

Instead, I could only look on in shame. He took the candy first, ate it with gusto. He sniffed the glass of water, wrinkled his nose and set the glass back down. He began opening cupboards, and when he found a glass bottle with brown liquid in it, he took a long swig.

He so near, but me so unable to move. Then I realized something I could do. He could see his way around the room because of me.

I needed to snuff myself out.

I strained and strained and shrugged and pushed but could not pull my wick inside.

He went back to the fireplace. I'd not noticed before but he'd brought in a large gray sack with him. He reached inside it and pulled out a parcel wrapped in paper as red as his suit and stuck it into the little girl's stocking hanging on the fireplace.

Whatever he'd put there, it had to be a trick. Something to explode like the candle man's powder, or perhaps he was spreading the weight of his belongings so he could steal the stocking, too, and use it to carry the fruits of his plunder. As if this poor family had anything to steal, they didn't even have a log for the fire. Shame really, if they had he would never have made it in.

I strained and shrugged and pushed again. This time a tad of wax shifted toward my wick. I paused in my efforts, rather impressed that I'd managed this much.

Now the man was redistributing his things into the boy's stocking. He'd leave the children legless.

I redoubled my efforts. I strained and shrugged and as if by magic, the wax flooded over my wick and I was out. I'd done it! It was dark. Well, a glow of moonlight came through the window, but pitifully dark if you'd asked me. Now the man would surely trip or bang into the table and wake the family, and all would be saved.

I waited for it, waited to hear him stumble. Only he didn't. He sat back down at the table and took three more long swigs of the brown stuff. He topped the bottle back up with water from the jug and set it back in the cupboard. All as though he could see just fine.

As I was puzzling the logic of all this, I almost missed the sound of him striding back across the room, a whisper and a swoosh and he was gone, through the chimney I presumed.

That was perhaps the grimmest moment of my life. Left in the dark. Itching and aching because of whatever grit was inside me. And with the knowledge that I'd let the family down. If I'd put myself out as soon as the red man had arrived, surely he wouldn't have been able to find the bottle in the cupboard, the stockings on the fireplace. The latter I was sure he swiped on his way out.

Unable to scratch my itches, defend the room from the dark, or reconcile my feelings of failure, I moped until, I confess, I drifted off. I've no way to tell how much time passed until whispers from the boy and girl roused me. They were by the fireplace; they must have found their stockings gone. They both came to the table and in the faint glimmer of moonlight I saw them set the stockings on it.

How could that be? I must have foiled the red man after all. He must have missed his swag on the way out in the dark.

The children had found some matches. The boy struck one in a swoosh of glare and I braced for the pinch of my wick. I felt it. Then I felt nothing. The match had gone out, I was not alight.

The boy struck another match, but again, a little pinch. I did not light. The wax! I'd spread it over my wick, so there was little chance he'd manage to light me. *Wiggle me out of the wax, cut my wax if you have to*—I would have told them if I could have said words.

The boy tried again. Again, to no avail. I heard him drop the matchbox on the table. I did not hear a rattle. He must have used the very last one.

This family had no wood, and now no matches. You might think I'd have rejoiced at the extra life I'd live if they couldn't light me, but the children's disappointment was tangible. Black and disappointing as the night. And all I'd ever wanted was a life well lived!

The children shuffled their stockings on the table, then the girl said, "I wish we had light."

Light. That would be me. I'd done what I could to save them from the red man, but in doing so I'd taken away their joy.

Then the boy said, "I wish we had light, too."

Two wishes, one failed candle.

It was their glum desolation that made me think of such an outlandish thought as I did next.

If I had snuffed myself out all on my own, surely there was a way for me to relight myself without a match.

Perhaps I could strain and strain and shrug and push and I'd spark right back up.

I strained and strained and shrugged and pushed. Nothing.

The girl picked me up. Her hands a bit rough, she set me on the plate where the candy no longer was. I waited, she waited. Nothing happened.

I tried again. Still nothing.

"Let's both hold it," the girl said, and I felt two pairs of small hands around me. "If we wish hard enough, perhaps he will light."

"I wish the candle to light," said the boy.

"I wish the candle to light," said the girl.

I strained and pushed. I felt a tickle in my wick.

"I believe," said the girl.

"I believe," said the boy.

I shrugged and strained one more time and thought with all my might, *I wish to light. I believe, I believe.*

I felt a pinch. Could it be?

The children squealed with delight. I'd done it! I would have squealed, too, if I could. To see the expressions of joy on their faces, flickering from the new flame on my wick!

The girl carried me to the chair near the fireplace, and sat scrunched up against her brother.

The boy had brought the packages from the stockings. He tore the paper carefully off one of them. Inside was a book. He held me next, and the girl took a turn at pulling the paper off the second package. Inside hers was a book also.

Next came the moment I'd cherish the most from my short life.

"Once upon a time..." the girl began. As she read, the two children snuggled closer and closer. Once in a while one of them gasped. A few times both of them laughed. The whole time I could see and hear and feel their joy.

And they were feeling that joy because of me. Well, because of the book, too, to give credit where credit's due.

Just as I was thinking my life could not have ended on a better note, I felt a frazzle. A flicker of a shoot of light. It was coming from my itchy insides. Another shoot of light and a flicker. A sizzling sound, too. The more I sizzled, the stronger the smell of cinnamon. Then more shoots and flickers, a dazzling display of magical darts of light. I was a light show! A fragrant one at that. I can't pretend to understand, but it had to be something to do with the gritty concoction the candle man had poured into me. I sizzled and shot and sparkled. The children were thrilled!

"Mom, Dad, come and see. It's magic!" they cried.

The parents seemed in just as much awe. The four of them huddled and hugged together, ooh-ing and aah-ing as the last bits of me propelled into the air, lighting their delighted faces. These two poor children, whose parents had not a single log of wood or a match left, who were unlikely to have more than a bowl of turnip water for dinner, whooped with delight and more joy than I ever knew could exist. And I had delivered it to them.

"Merry Christmas," the mother said.

"Merry Christmas," the others echoed.

The last sweet words I heard. My life, in the end, well spent.

THE CHRISTMAS TREE

Kathleen Shoop

1861

Night fell. Elmer Barnes' breath came quick and shallow. He collapsed to his knees as though doing so would allow him to shelter under the whipping gales. Snow sank through his trousers, icing his knees. He dug through the crisp, heavy layers, removed his gloves, and scraped his fingers against the frozen dirt. His dirt. Torn apart by a tornado, then re-sown with corn, desperate prayers, and tears. Yield: Nothing. Stubborn for only the second time since he'd bought his beloved patch of earth. Betraying. How could this be? Nothing to sell that year...

A loan from his friend around the bend near the lake had dissolved like day into night when Elmer's brother came calling for the same money. Elmer's wife, Bea, insisted they give it to him, that his family needed it more. Elmer's breath stopped at the thought of Bea. He squeezed his eyes shut, fighting to start breathing again. Oh god, her eyes when he told her there would be no seed to sow in the spring... the sight of her forcing a smile, turning away, toward her stove so she could wipe her tears, thinking he wouldn't notice, that he would have already turned his attention to their sons, Adam and Clyde, and not witnessed her disappointment. He thought a hundred times that Bea's constant generosity had been a mistake. If only they'd kept a little bit back for themselves.

He didn't need to see her tears to know they were there. Disillusionment wrapped Bea like the woolen coat she wore to trudge through sleety blizzards to share eggs with needy neighbors. Now the Barneses were needy. The failure to harvest tore at Elmer because he'd broken the promise he made to Bea's father when they emigrated to the United States. "Riches, land, endless crops," he'd said with his chest pushed out, chin up, his pride ballooning so big they could have sailed on it across the Atlantic.

Yet here they were with nothing. Three weeks until Christmas. And there was nothing.

Elmer didn't know how long he knelt there, but when he started to rise, his breath was snatched away yet again. The clouds had cleared. All around, stars blinked in the sapphire heavens. Light winked through piney boughs, drawing his gaze this way then that. Massive, ancient pines waved, branches flapping in the wind like great birds preparing to take off. And then he saw it. A star shot from the left, tracking over the treetops. For a moment it hovered, like a summer butterfly, aweing him to the point he nearly forgot to wish on it.

Please, please, please. Send me an answer. Send me a way to buy the seed we need for spring, to keep my family.

Back in the house, Bea dashed toward Elmer, wrapping him tight, his size dwarfing hers. She pulled back, rubbed his arms and back, heating him up. "Adam's adding blankets to the beds. Tonight's especially cold... well you know, you were just..." she looked down at his wet knees. "What were you doing?"

He didn't answer.

"I know you don't believe me," she said. "But I'm not worried. We'll survive. More than that. I just know it."

He swallowed hard, marveling at her hopeful gaze, her steadfast words hanging between them.

"The world's forces have decided differently." He thought of all the ways he could parcel the land, to sell it in pieces so they could keep the house and make a go of the remaining acreage.

She pulled him toward the table near the fire and spread out the newspaper. "Here. Laura gave me this in trade, said the news of the day would take your mind off things."

"Always does." He squeezed Bea's hand. "Thank her for me."

She brushed her fingertips over the back of his head, comforting him. Their neighbor always passed along the papers when she didn't have money for eggs. Elmer sipped Bea's hot coffee, finishing the pot. Article after article lifted his mood or deepened his dejection.

He studied the front page illustration of a boy and his father yanking an enormous pine tree through a wood, smiling.

"Shame," Bea poked at the paper. She went to the window. "Couldn't imagine trading a lifetime of seeing a tree through each and every season just to have it in my house for a few days at Christmas."

Elmer read aloud from the article. "Makes us feel like all is right in the world when we decorate our tree. It's beauty unrivaled right in our own home. A little bit of decadence for a little bit of time..."

Bea sighed. "Not sure 'bout that."

In the bedroom Elmer pushed the curtain aside and gazed into the night. Pointing to the huge tree in front, the one the shooting star had hovered over, he slipped an arm around Bea and pulled her close. She shivered as a breeze worked through the window seal. Before she could pull the curtain closed, he stopped her. "Really. Look, Bea. Look at this beauty. I saw a falling star right over that tree, just hung there, the other ones all glimmering through the boughs and above and..."

"I saw it," she said barely above a whisper. "Wished on it."

"Me too," he said.

They stared at each other for a moment, energy coursing between them, filling him with fresh love, new understanding of what he'd built with his wife over the years.

He ran his finger along her jaw, her skin softer than anything he'd ever touched. "I understand why those people want to bring nature into their homes for a couple weeks. Even for a moment." He looked back out the window. "This beauty. It's all ours... I understand." He choked on the thought they could lose it, that next year it might be them dragging a tree into their house for a few days of beauty at Christmas.

She got up on her toes and pulled his face down to hers, kissing him. "You're a good soul, Elmer. And I see exactly what you mean."

She reached for the curtain again.

"Leave it," he said.

"Too cold," she said.

"I'll keep you warm." He smiled down on her, laying his forehead against hers.

Elmer and Bea leapt out of bed before sunrise. When she finished with the chamber pot and washed up, Elmer tossed her an old pair of Adam's pants and a thick cable-knit sweater.

"Wind's wailing right through the walls. Can't have you getting the eggs with that chill working up your skirt."

She laughed as she dressed and found a bit of rope to tie around her waist to keep the pants up. "I knew I picked the right man when I chose you over Matthew Stone." They hurried to the door for their boots—standing largest to smallest—but Bea's had shifted from the second pair, all the way to the end as though she were now a child. Wedging her feet into hers, she whispered, "Matthew Stone would've had me traipsing around in silken shoes, lacy drawers flapping in the wind."

Elmer chuckled and pulled her close. "At least you'd have silken shoes and lacy drawers... He'd have hired hands to do all of this work... He'd..."

She put her finger over his lips. "Don't want any of that."

The scent of her honey soap filled him. He relaxed and took her hands. "I love you, Bea. I love you so much." He hoped love could fill in the gaps the lack of seed would leave in their life.

She wrapped a red scarf around her neck and a blue one around his. "And I love you."

The two of them headed into the weather, toward the barn and henhouse, the stillness broken by their feet crunching through fresh snow. As they passed the back of the house Elmer saw a golden glow behind the boys' bedroom curtain. They'd risen for their chores.

Back inside with chores completed, four sets of boots again stood by the door. Elmer drank tea as Bea pushed eggs onto everyone's plates. "Can't believe how many the girls gave me today, being so cold. Plenty to take to the Joneses and the Mayhews."

Elmer grimaced but kept quiet. He loved her benevolence but they were no longer in a position to give so much. But her kindness—the way it made her feel— might be the only Christmas gift she received this year and so he let her be.

Clyde and Adam opened yesterday's newspaper between them, chattering as they read.

"Fifty cents apiece?" Adam said. "Who'd pay that for a dead tree?"

Clyde nodded. "Save that money to buy the land that grows the trees. Then you'll have something."

"I always wanted to make a go of it in New York City," Adam said. "But not if I've got to check my brain at the ferry."

"Yeah, I can see having a decorated tree in town for everyone to enjoy, but in your own house?" Clyde asked.

Adam drew his finger under the words as he read. "Says here they head out to a farm, cut the tree, haul the tree... they could have made fifty cents in the time it took them to fetch a piney carcass."

"Fifty non-sense," Clyde scoffed.

"Insane. Who'd be so stupid?" Adam said.

Elmer noticed Bea looking out the window, hands wrapped around her teacup. He didn't like to see her sad.

"What if..." she said something Elmer couldn't hear.

"What, Mum?" Adam said.

She shook her head and sipped her tea, staring out the window.

"What if..." Bea looked as though she were conversing with herself.

"Bea?" Elmer said.

She turned slowly, grinning. Was the cold weather and bleak prospects turning her mad?

"We've so much more than our share."

Elmer and the boys glanced at each other. "Share of troubles, sure."

She sauntered toward them, put her teacup down and traced her finger over the front page illustration. "Says right there, New Yorkers are spending entire days traveling to the country, cutting a tree, hauling it back, sticking it in their homes..."

Clyde straightened in his chair. "For fifty cents."

Elmer was starting to understand what Bea was saying. "No, no, Bea. Those are like our babies."

She nodded. "And eventually some babies fly the coop."

"It's one thing to travel to Brooklyn to cut a tree. No one's traveling here. Eighty miles or so..." Elmer said.

"Well, maybe," Adam said.

"Cross the Hudson..." Clyde said.

"For a tree. No way," Elmer said.

"We'd be better off collecting pinecones and hauling them to the city to sell so people could grow their own trees."

"That's it, Adam," Bea said. "That's the idea."

Elmer's brow furrowed. "What?"

She bit her lip and held his gaze.

She couldn't be serious. "No, Bea."

She went to the window. Elmer joined her there. They stared at the trees that hugged their home. Elmer tried to visualize how many they owned, how they funneled out, deep and wide to the Hudson River, curving back into the mountains. Thousands of trees. Thousands. He calculated the time it would take to cut and tie and load and haul and travel to New York. Imagine if those same New Yorkers only had to walk ten or twenty blocks to get their Christmas tree... they'd pay... he couldn't even imagine.

But it was a terrible idea.

He looked at Bea whose eyes were lit like the sun as she stared out the window and sipped her tea.

"What was your wish on the shooting star last night?" he asked.

She turned to him, still grinning, but not answering.

It was then he knew. They'd wished on the same star, same wish. Neither said a word, but both knew in their bones this was the solution to their sorrows, the echo of the hopes, their silent pleas.

Adam and Clyde joined their parents at the window. Clyde pointed. "I can't believe it came true."

Elmer, Adam and Bea stared at him.

"What came true?" Elmer asked.

"My wish. Wished upon a falling star... right there. Above that one."

Adam scoffed. "That was my star. My wish."

"Mine...."

"What did you all wish for?" Bea said, her face full of wonder.

"For a way to—" Clyde said.

Elmer gripped his shoulder. "Shush. No. Don't say it aloud."

And the four of them fell into each other, hugging for dear life, each hoping this crazy wish-fueled idea might actually work, that this answer would bring their spring seed and turn everything right again.

They rushed to ready for the trip, working daylight into darkness, with Bea holding two lamps to illuminate the area. Selecting, chopping, and wrapping the boughs tight made Elmer cringe with every act of "rudeness" to the once living beauties. Cording the boughs felt like roping his sons' arms and legs to their bodies. Yet it was the only answer. They figured they could haul forty trees safely and in time for families to buy for Christmas. Once everything was loaded, Bea fitted several baskets of food into the wagon behind the seat.

Elmer held her close, his lips brushing her ear, her skin salty. "We'll take care, we'll be safe, we'll save our farm."

She clung hard, nodding into his chest. "I already know."

The trip took the three Barnes men, their oxen, wagon and trees through rutted mountain passes. They traded turns sleeping, eating, and chopping their way through sections too overgrown and impassable for the full to bursting wagon. Once it lurched sideways onto two wheels, sending four trees over the ridge. Only thirty-six trees left to sell.

Halfway to Washington Market in New York City, they descended from the mountains and moved quickly over open roads. This segment lightened their moods and had them imagining how much they'd charge for each tree and what they'd then plant that spring.

"Fifty cents at least," Adam said. "We're saving them the trip out of town."

"Then charge more," Clyde said.

"More? For dead trees? I love Christmas as much as anyone, but... I don't know."

Elmer let them banter about pricing. He'd wait until they surveyed the market, saw what other greenery was offered. Was it possible no one else thought to do this? He worried they'd arrive with these stunning trees—trees that broke his heart with every chop—and no one would buy them, that no one would ever enjoy their splendor. He flinched every time he imagined Bea's face if he had to tell her their wishes hadn't been answered at all.

He stopped himself from sad thoughts and swallowed his doubts. Instead, he focused on the shooting star, the way it had hung over the mammoth tree closest to the house, how they all wished together, all for the same exact thing.

Elmer pulled into the ferry station and a thrill coursed through him. The boys rubbed their hands together, excited to be so close to purchasing vendor space and making their dreams come true.

The ferryman scratched some information on a paper and handed it to Elmer. His mind flew as he read the note. He added then recalculated the freight cost. "This right?"

The ferryman nodded. "Pay up and move. Wagons lined clear to the ocean behind you."

Elmer pulled his coins out. He knew he needed the silver dollar for the vendor space. But they had underestimated the cost for the freight. It was the last bit of money they had.

The ferryman wiggled his fingers at Elmer, palm up.

Clyde hopped out of the wagon. "Adam and I'll wait here."

"But..."

Adam patted his father's leg. "Go. Sell those trees."

Elmer calculated again, another way. They couldn't risk the vendor fees being higher than estimated, either. Adam was already out of the wagon with some of the food Bea packed by the time Elmer looked at them. Their faces were chapped but bright with faith. Just like their mother.

"Wait right there. One way or another I'll be back on the last ferry."

And so he went.

The silver dollar paid Elmer's way into the market. He pulled his wagon to the corner of Greenwich and Vesey, stomach flipping and churning. What if no one wanted his trees? Dozens of sellers were set up with boughs of holly and pine, but no one boasted a rig full of emerald magic. Still, hours passed and no one even asked what he was doing with a load of tied up trees. Hungry, he opened the third basket Bea had packed. He gasped. It was full of red and green bows, paper snowflakes, and a star made from tin with charming, uneven sides.

Tucked into the ribbons was a note.

While you were cutting trees, I made ornaments that will show people who never bought a tree why they should...

He yanked a pine from the wagon, stood it up, and released the limbs with a flop and a whoosh as the tree exhaled. He added the decorations then stood on the edge of the wagon to top the tree with the tin star. It caught the afternoon sunrays, making him squint at the brilliance. It shone like their shooting star, making him wish his family was there to witness it.

He hopped down and wiped his hands against his pants. The tree was a beautiful example of what he saw every time he looked out his window. He stroked one bough. "You'll make a family very happy."

Someone tapped his shoulder.

"How much?"

With all the hubbub at the ferry station, Elmer had forgotten about pricing. He inhaled, thought of the article, about the joy the trees brought those who took one into their home, the magic they brought him every single day, the work it took to haul them from home and before he could stop himself, he blurted it out.

"One dollar."

The man scowled.

Elmer wanted to bite the number back. "These are special trees."

The man slid his gaze over the gorgeous example Elmer had arranged by the wagon.

"Shooting star went right overhead of this bunch. Sprinkled with genuine stardust."

"Fine, fine. The wife will jump for joy when I bring one of these home. Told her there was no way we could make it to Brooklyn this year just for a tree."

"Tell her, not just any tree. A Christmas tree brought from a stand of trees where shooting stars..."

"Yeah," the man said. "All of that."

Back home, Elmer, Adam, and Clyde scrambled into the arms of Bea. Tears flowed down her cheeks as she peeked into the back of the wagon. "Tell me they didn't just fall out in the mountain pass."

Elmer and the boys passed mischievous smiles. "Well..."

"No..." Bea said,

"Just four tumbled out."

"Mama," Clyde pulled a canvas sack from his coat pocket and put it in his mother's palm. She lifted it up and down, her mouth dropping open.

"How much?"

"One dollar," Adam said.

Her eyebrows went up.

"Per tree—" Clyde said.

"A whole dollar?" She screeched like never before.

"And the tree with all the decorations you made went for three dollars."

She slapped her hands over her mouth. "That was supposed to go free to someone special. Did you read the whole note?"

Elmer nodded. "He was special. He insisted on paying."

"I can't... I just... I..."

"I know, I know," the boys jumped up and down.

"Go on and water the oxen," Elmer said, watching them drive the wagon to the barn, pointing to the trees as they went, their voices piercing the still night.

Elmer looked back at Bea and they fell together. He picked her up and swung her, the bag of coins smacking him in the back, clinking. He didn't know how to fully express his love for her.

They stood staring at the pines, the joy that swelled him making him wonder how he got so lucky.

Bea leaned her head on his shoulder. "Now we can afford to plant *and* give the Smiths that cow they need."

Elmer flinched. How could they possibly give away a cow like it was nothing? They would still have to float the original loan until his brother could pay on it. He opened his mouth to disagree but the pines gently swaying in the wind stopped him.

Open your eyes.

The trees, the wishes, the prayers. All of it had provided, protected his family, giving them an unimaginable gift.

Bea shifted in Elmer's arms, her warmth dizzying him, filling him like nothing else. And in that moment, a wave of realization swept through him.

He'd been wrong.

It wasn't the desperate wishing upon a shooting star that brought them their riches, it was all the giving Bea did every single day that gave them clarity, that brought the newspaper to them and changed everything. He pulled her closer, his chin on her head, grateful for her more than anything else in the world. All of the nothing that had been theirs the week before was now more than they could share in a lifetime. And to see that, to feel it, was everything. Their hopes realized in an instant.

NOTE: Inspired by the true tale of Mark Carr, the first farmer to sell Christmas trees in Washington Market, NYC.

TINK

Abigail Drake

I hate reindeer.

Oh, I know. Everyone assumes they are these sweet, jolly, magical creatures.

Newsflash: that's Santa. Reindeer suck, and taking care of them sucked, too.

Of all the jobs at the North Pole, this was one of the worst. Cleaning out the stalls, organizing all their freaking games, making sure their jingle bells sparkled in the moonlight. Who cares about shiny jingle bells? Reindeer provided nothing more than a means to an end. Santa had to deliver gifts to a bunch of ungrateful human spawn, and the reindeer helped him do this.

Actually, we all helped him. Every single elf living in the North Pole spent the entirety of their existence working toward one common goal—making and distributing toys to children who would forget all about them a week after Christmas.

Utterly meaningless, and I hated every minute of it. I didn't disguise my feelings, either. One little snarky comment about where a child could stick his toy train, and I got cut from my position in the letter reading department and reassigned to this. Poop duty.

"Hey, Tinklebelle Holly. I've got a little itch. Can you scratch it for me?" asked Comet, lifting his leg to show me one of his giant... well, it wasn't a jingle bell.

They loved calling me by my full name, even though everyone else who valued their life called me Tink. And the reindeer also loved showing me their balls for some reason. It felt like working in a high school locker room. It smelled like that, too.

"Tink. I need to speak with you. Now." Puck McHappy, the burly manager of the reindeer division, indicated the door to his office with a filthy finger.

"What?" I followed him inside, wiping the powdery white dust off my orange coveralls. I had no idea where it came from, but I went home every day covered in it. Yet another perk to the reindeer gig.

Puck leaned back in his chair and hefted his feet onto the desk. His boots, covered in reindeer feces, made me want to gag.

In spite of the gross factor, I liked Puck. He was fair, direct, great in a bar fight, and always good for a laugh, but he wasn't laughing now.

"This just came in." He tossed a paper at me over the desk. I caught it just before it hit his dirty boots. "You've been reassigned."

Last week, I'd applied for my dream job, a position overseeing the naughty list, and hope burgeoned in my chest. No more looking at Comet's hairy testicles? No more smelling Donner's farts? No more inappropriate comments from Vixen? Vixen was a scumbag, by the way. I caught him playing some reindeer games with Dancer's wife at the company pre-Christmas party. I wanted to pour bleach into my eyes.

"I knew you were too pretty to last here. Too sparkly, too, even for a Christmas elf. With that hair." He indicated my blonde hair. I tucked a lock of it behind my pointy ear, self-consciously.

"What about my hair?"

He sighed, scratching his big belly. What was it with males and scratching? Were they perpetually itchy or something? The only reindeer who didn't scratch, and wasn't a complete asshole, was Rudolph. But Rudolph was... well, let me just say, flying was the only thing that guy did straight.

Wink, wink.

"It's not just your hair," said Puck. "It's also your boobs and everything."

I looked down at my chest. My boobs didn't look any different from anyone else's boobs. I opened my mouth to ask him what was wrong with them, but he waved a hand to shut me up.

"This isn't about your boobs. I'm sorry I brought them up." He checked his watch. "You're to report to the main office. You'd better scoot."

"Thanks, Puck," I said.

"Be careful out there, kiddo," he said, and I hugged him, filthy fingers and all.

I ran back to my apartment as fast as my elfin feet would carry me. After taking a quick shower, I put on a short skirt and heels. The skirt was a precaution. I had nice legs, and anything that would get me out of the reindeer department was useful at this point.

I made it to the main office in record time. A large clock on the wall indicated the countdown to the big day, and people rushed around, doing important things. Only one month to go, and everyone felt the pressure.

"Ms. Holly?" The receptionist's eyes narrowed disapprovingly at the length of my skirt. I attempted to pull it down discreetly as she ushered me into a large office, but as soon as I saw the man sitting behind the big, shiny desk, my heart sank.

Cookie Wassail. The same man who'd fired me from my job in the letter writing department. And the packaging team. And the distribution center. And the elfin relations department.

I shook his hand, hoping my palms weren't sweaty. "Mr. Wassail. Nice to see you again."

He leaned back in his chair and indicated I should sit down. "I wish I could say the same, Tinklebelle."

I swallowed hard. "Am I in trouble, sir?"

He sighed, and I knew this sound well, since I'd heard it many times before. "There have been complaints. From the reindeer."

"Is this about Comet's balls?" I asked, fury rising in my chest.

"Uh, no," he said, blinking in surprise. "This is about your attitude, or, rather, your 'baditude.' Why can't you just smile and be happy like the other elves? Every word that comes out of your mouth is either an insult or a complaint."

"It is not—" I began, but Cookie interrupted me.

"Enough. I'm not going to punish you. I called you here to give you an opportunity. You recently applied for a job on the naughty list team, correct?"

I nodded, almost afraid to speak. Was I getting fired or hired? I had no idea.

Cookie studied my face. "I want to give you a chance, but you're going to have to prove yourself."

I narrowed my eyes at him. "How?"

"This morning, someone showed up from Elfin High Council to conduct a surprise audit. We don't like surprises." He adjusted his glasses. "He needs a tour guide, and you've worked in nearly every department in the North Pole. Who could be better? Also, you're smart enough to show him only what we want him to see. If you can manage not to mess this up, the position you applied for is yours. If not, you'll be reassigned. To the coal mines. Am I clear?"

"Crystal." No one assigned to the coal mines ever left. It was a life sentence and we both knew it.

"Good," he said, just as a knock came at the door. "Here he is now."

I turned around to see who I'd have to play nice with for the next few days, expecting a balding bureaucrat, but instead I got a big surprise. The guy was a dark elf.

I'd just been set up. Holy roasted chestnuts. This would not end well.

Each of the elfin tribes was made up of members of the same ancient, magical species. There were the cookie making elves, the gardening elves (they tended to be naked a lot), the shoemaking elves... and the dark ones. No one liked the dark elves. They lived in caves and weren't the kind of elves you invited to cocktail parties. Or any parties. They were scary.

Cookie spoke, snapping me out of my stupor. "Tinklebelle Holly, this is Jax Grayson."

Jax Grayson's eyes met mine and I had to force myself not to stare. A dark elf working for the High Council? This was unusual, but everything about this guy was unusual. And intriguing. And, well, sexy. Okay, fine. I'll admit it. The guy was one hot elf.

"Nice to meet you, Mr. Grayson," I said, and curtsied. Like I was meeting the queen.

His lips quirked in amusement. "Please call me Jax."

My cheeks got hot as he held my gaze. Jax Grayson was not at all what I expected. This could mean trouble.

Cookie handed me a thin, red folder. "I've prepared a detailed itinerary."

I opened it up, my eyes scanning the pages. Something felt off here. I didn't know what, but if my choices were between showing a good-looking guy around for a few days, or going to the coal mines, I'd take the good-looking guy.

I led Jax to the accounting department, the first stop on Cookie's itinerary. I showed him the room full of elves tapping away on their computers and tried to disguise the fact that most played online games instead of doing actual work. Jax asked intelligent questions, and I answered as honestly as I could. I kind of liked the guy, which was why it bothered me that the other elves whispered about him behind his back. When a woman named Plum Pudding (that is seriously her name), let out a squawk of alarm when she saw him, I shook my head in disgust.

"I'm sorry," I said. "They've never seen a dark elf before."

"I guess I stand out."

Members of the various elfin tribes had notably different physical attributes. Christmas elves tended to be cute and sparkly. The cookie-making ones were a little on the heavy side, for obvious reasons. The shoemakers were short, mean, and drank a lot. The garden elves looked like garden gnomes, but since they hated both clothing and societal rules, they tended to be a bit promiscuous. The High Council elves, and the others living in Elf Central, were the brightest and best from each of the different tribes, so they were normally full of themselves. And the dark elves were, well, dark. Dark hair, dark eyes, dark aura of darkness.

Jax had the dark elf coloring, and the aura, but he was not a typical High Council elf at all. He exuded confidence, not arrogance, and, well, he wasn't a prick.

"Have you ever seen a dark elf before, Tinklebelle?" he asked, looking at me out of the corner of his eye.

"Nope. You're my first. And please call me Tink. I hate being called Tinklebelle. It makes me sound so fluffy and vapid and Christmas-y."

"You don't want to be Christmas-y?"

"No, I'm not a fan," I said, feeling the old familiar pang in my heart.

"A Christmas elf who isn't into Christmas?" He studied my face with a hint of amusement in his eyes. "You're unusual, Tink."

"What do you mean?"

"Well, you didn't scream and run away when you saw me."

"Don't flatter yourself," I said, unable to resist. "I've seen far scarier things than you—"

My words were cut off by a scream coming from the atrium just outside the accounting department. Jax and I turned to see a woman convulsing on the ground, blood trickling out of her nose, mouth, and her pretty pointy ears.

Christmas elves were not good in an emergency. We tended to run around and scream a lot, which was what most of the other elves did right now. I'd never been one to panic, but as I knelt next to the woman and grabbed her clammy hand, I had to fight the urge not to run around and scream, too.

I knew this elf. I'd worked with her.

Jax placed his fingers on her neck to check her pulse, and frowned. "Call the medics, Tink. Now."

I did as he asked, and Elf Medical Team arrived only a few minutes later, but it was already too late. I stayed next to her as they tried to revive her, but there was nothing they could do.

"Her name was Joy Berry," I said softly as they carried her off on a gurney, a white sheet covering her face. "She worked with me in the reindeer division. She always brought an extra muffin for me in case I forgot to eat breakfast. What happened to her?"

"She died from a drug overdose." He looked down at me, his dark eyes steady. "Candicocane."

I'd heard about the candicocane problem on the news, but never involving a Christmas elf. We didn't do the hard stuff. Our idea of a fun time was drinking hot cocoa spiked with too much peppermint schnapps. Yes, it made you puke, but it didn't make you die.

And Joy wasn't the type, even for the peppermint schnapps, and I told Jax as much. "Joy wouldn't even take a pain pill from me when she had cramps. This doesn't make sense."

My skirt had flecks of Joy's blood on it. It made me want to cry.

"Come on," he said, grabbing my hand and helping me to my feet. "Let's go somewhere quiet and talk."

I took him to my favorite bar, Nick's, and we sat alone in a booth in the corner. I ordered my usual. He ordered whisky on the rocks, which seemed somehow appropriate for a dark elf.

When our drinks arrived, he studied my neon green concoction with a raised eyebrow. "What is that?"

"The Grinch," I said, taking a long sip. "It's disgusting, but I like it. I think of the Grinch as my spirit animal."

His lips curved into a smile. "You really do hate this Christmas stuff, don't you?"

"I really do."

"To the Grinch." He raised his glass, and after we both drank deeply, he leaned closer. "Tell me more about your friend Joy."

I shrugged. "I didn't know her well, but she's a nice kid." I blinked away tears. "Was a nice kid, I mean."

"Did she ever talk to you about problems with her job?"

I shook my head. "No, but there has to be a reason you're asking me this."

He stared at me, as if weighing his words. "I'm not here to do an audit."

"I guessed as much. So, what's a nice boy like you doing in a place like this?"

He gave me a crooked smile. "I'm here to investigate the recent surge in candicocane-related deaths. You saw what happened to your friend. That's becoming a daily occurrence, and the body count is mounting."

"Why?"

He held my gaze, his expression grim. "Someone has been lacing candicocane with telazol and distributing it throughout all the elfin communities."

I frowned. "Reindeer tranquilizer?"

"Yes," he said. "And we've figured out it's all coming from the North Pole."

I stayed so calm, I impressed myself. With the wave of a hand, I ordered another Grinch, then focused all of my slightly inebriated attention on the elf in front of me. "Who are you, Jax Grayson? I'd like to know the truth this time."

He hesitated only a moment before taking out a badge from the inside pocket of his suit. It shone in the dim light of the bar. "Elf Enforcement, narcotics division."

"Oh," I said. "A dark narc."

He grinned, and it did funny and unexpected things to my elfin nether regions. "You may have had one Grinch too many. Let's eat something, and then we'll talk."

Jax ordered food and coffee for both of us and filled me in on the details. "Someone is secretly transporting large amounts of the telazol-laced candicocane all over the world. They're employing some sort of magic to do it, but it's not showing up on our radar so we can't track it. We got a tip a few days ago that it was coming from here. I was supposed to meet with the tipster, but now I can't."

"Why?"

His eyes met mine. "Because she's dead."

"Joy?" I sat back in my seat, shaking my head.

"Someone killed her to keep her quiet," he said. "And made it look like an overdose."

I pictured Joy's pale, lifeless face, and the blood trickling from her ears. She deserved better. "What can I do to help?"

He studied me carefully. "You knew Joy. You know a lot about this entire place. You're familiar with the reindeer department," he said. "But are you sure you want to get involved? This could be very dangerous."

"They killed my friend. She was just a kid. Yes, I want to help. I want to stop them before they kill someone else." I lifted my chin a little higher, faking a bravado I didn't actually feel.

He blew out a breath and got to his feet. "Then let's go," he said, helping me into my coat. "We have a few stops left on that oh-so-carefully prepared itinerary."

I frowned. "You think Cookie is involved?"

"I can't be certain, but I do know one thing. He assigned you to be my tour guide for one reason alone. He chose the prettiest elf he could think of because he wanted to distract me. He's hiding something, and I want to know what it is."

I still reeled from the "prettiest elf" comment, but I had an idea. I mentioned it as we made our way to the reindeer department. "You talked about a distribution system, and Joy was your informant. Would candicocane leave behind a white, dusty sort of residue?"

He nodded. "I suppose."

"Because I came home every day from work covered in the stuff. We all did."

"How well do you know Puck McHappy?"

I frowned at him. "You think he's involved?"

"He does have a record."

"That was nothing." I rolled my eyes. "Puck got into a fight one night over a bet. It was stupid. He was provoked..." I stopped walking as the implications clicked in my mind.

"What is it, Tink?"

"Puck isn't a criminal mastermind, but I know who is."

"Who?"

"Think about it, Jax. Who could carry drugs without setting off the magic radar system? Who could secretly distribute something to elves all over the world? Who would have access to telazol?" When he didn't answer, I continued. "It's the freaking reindeer."

He frowned. "Led by Puck?"

I shook my head. "No. Comet is the ring leader, I'm sure of it. And he's going to wish he never asked me to scratch those giant, hairy balls of his."

That stopped Jax in his tracks. "Excuse me?"

"It's a long story," I said. "But we'd better hurry. The moon is just rising in the sky. That's when their magic is at its strongest. If my hunch is correct, those reindeer are about to head out on another drug run, and we need to catch them in the act."

Jax called for back-up, and the entire North Pole Police Force showed up at the reindeer paddock just after we did. This was not as impressive as it sounded. The NPPF consisted of about a dozen sparkly elves in powder blue uniforms, but they were intimidating enough that Comet didn't put up a fight when we caught him with bags of candicocane strapped to his back. Within minutes, Vixen confessed, and so did Prancer. With just a little prodding, they also gave the name of a certain elf who'd accepted bribes to turn a blind eye to their activities. Cookie Wassail got arrested the next day, and Jax let me be there when it happened.

The scandal caused shock waves to go through the entire North Pole community. A few weeks later, on Christmas Eve, I got a special commendation from Santa for my efforts. Jax came back from Elf Central to watch me receive it. It was a big deal.

Santa climbed onto the podium, his eyes twinkling as he regarded the crowd. "I'd like to present this award to Tinklebelle Holly, for outstanding bravery and remarkable intuition. Thank you for a job well done."

I shook Santa's gloved hand and smiled for the cameras as Jax grinned at me from the front row. Then, to my surprise, Santa pulled me aside for a private word.

"How are you holding up, Tinklebelle? I know this time of year isn't easy for you."

"I'm fine," I said, glancing at the clock. "You'd better go. Tonight's your big night."

"I have time for this. It's important." He stared deeply into my eyes. "Your parents were good elves. The accident wasn't your fault, you know."

I flinched, remembering the crash, the breaking glass, the sounds of my mother's screams, the blood. "I don't blame myself."

His expression turned sad. "You blame Christmas."

"I did. For a long time. But I think this year will be different. I'm feeling oddly festive."

"Because of the job overseeing the naughty list? It's yours if you want it, you know. You deserve it."

"Thanks, Santa, but I have other plans." I pulled out the gold badge from inside my coat pocket. "Elf Enforcement. Special Agent Holly. Christmas Crimes Division. The reindeer were just the tip of the iceberg. It's time to clean up the North Pole, and I'm just the elf to do it."

LIMITED TIME OFFER

Phil Giunta

Cast iron hinges groaned in protest as Derek opened the door of the secluded country house and gestured for Kristy to precede him out to the porch. He adjusted his sunglasses and gazed at the surrounding fields, dappled with patches of melting snow under an unblemished cerulean sky. *The kind that only winter can provide. Beautiful job as always, Dakota.*

"Derek, this place is enormous. I can't imagine what it's costing you to rent it."

"Would you stop worrying about money? It's the holidays. Besides, I'd pay almost anything to get away from our crazy families for a few days."

"True that. Christmas dinner was awkward as hell." Kristy zipped up her coat and slipped on her gloves. "Did it get colder out here since we arrived?" The stinging chill of the occasional breeze foretold an approaching snow squall, but Derek knew it wouldn't arrive until after midnight. At least, that was the plan. "So, what did you want to show me?"

Derek stepped off the porch and nodded toward the tree line at the edge of the property. "It's a surprise. You'll just have to trust me."

"You're not taking me to some dark corner of the woods to kill me, are you?"

Derek smirked. "I can think of far more fun things to do with you in the dark, hot stuff."

Kristy leapt from the porch and into his arms. "Promises, promises."

The entire mountain range was ablaze—or so it appeared as the sun dipped low in the western sky, bathing snow-capped peaks in a deep saffron glow. Derek cast a furtive glance at Kristy, her face radiant, eyes glistening.

"This is stunning," she whispered, as if anything louder would shatter the perfect moment.

"My thoughts exactly." Derek shoved a hand into the pocket of his coat. "You know, after we opened all of our Christmas presents yesterday, I realized there was one that I forgot to give you."

As Kristy turned toward him, Derek lowered himself to one knee and opened the small white box to reveal an engagement ring. "Young bachelor seeks beautiful maiden with whom to share a lifetime of romantic sunsets. Any takers?"

"Oh my God!" Kristy covered her gaping mouth for a moment before wiping her eyes. "As long as we can go someplace warm for our honeymoon."

"I was thinking tropical."

Kristy yanked off her glove and extended her left hand. "Deal."

Derek slipped the ring onto her finger and kissed the back of her hand. "I need to stand up. The ground is freezing."

Kristy glanced down at the dark stain covering his knee. "And wet."

Derek chuckled. "Yeah, I didn't think that part through. I was too nervous about popping the ques— "

She pulled him close and kissed him until he was nearly out of breath. "As if I would've said no."

"Well, that would have made our dinner reservation awkward. Let's get back to the house before it gets dark. Apparently, I need to change before we go out."

Kristy held up her hand as she started down the trail. "This diamond is huge. I can't imagine what you paid for it."

Derek was about to reply when the snow atop one of the distant peaks swirled and shifted. *That never happened before.* At first, it appeared to be the beginning of an avalanche—until several meters of the mountaintop flickered in and out of existence before solidifying once more.

"Something wrong?"

Derek turned to Kristy. "Uh, no. Just taking one last look."

Hand in hand, they headed back through the woods. Derek cast a final glance over his shoulder. *Don't ruin this on me, Dakota.*

At the Summit Steakhouse an hour later, the hostess seated them at a window table toward the back corner beside an elegant white Christmas tree illuminated by a string of blue lights. At each table, red and green candles in hurricane glasses complemented the dim ambient lighting. The rustic stained wood interior was reminiscent of a luxurious log home complete with crackling stone fireplace. From the ceiling speakers, Bing Crosby crooned "I'll Be Home for Christmas."

"This is cozy," Kristy said. "Our own private corner. Very romantic." She glanced up from the menu to peer through the window, but there was little to see beyond the exterior lights of the restaurant. "And the scenery is breathtaking."

Derek laughed. Situated atop the smallest of the mountains, the Summit was renowned for its unobstructed and breathtaking view of the entire valley—during the day, of course. "We'll come back for lunch later in the week. Trust me, it's a sight to behold, and you'll be able to say, 'I can see my house from here' because the place we're renting is," he pointed toward the bottom corner of the window, "just down there to the right."

"I look forward to it." Kristy returned to the menu. "Since you know this place, what do you recommend?"

"Well, the last time I—" As Derek scanned the appetizer page, the text vanished in a downward wipe. It was immediately replaced with a message.

Mr. Marcus, we apologize for the technical difficulty earlier at the lake. A severe ice storm has moved into the area and disrupted the power grid in our section of town. We appreciate your patience as we switch to backup power. We will do our best to minimize any further anomalies. Thank you and Merry Christmas. —Management

"Derek, you okay?"

He gazed at her over the top of his menu. "Uh, yeah. Sorry. The menu seems to have changed a bit since the last time I was here, but the Skillet Chicken Monterey is amazing."

"Good evening, folks."

Derek and Kristy glanced up at the waitress as she placed two glasses of water on the table. "My name is—"

"Dakota!" Derek blurted. "What are you doing here?"

"I work here, Mr. Marcus. You know that."

"Uh, yeah, right, of course. I just, uh, didn't expect you to be *here* tonight. Don't you normally go home over Christmas?"

"Not since my parents died. I'm on my own for the holidays, so might as well earn some money."

Once Dakota had taken their drink orders and was out of earshot, Kristy leaned forward. "What was that all about?"

"What do you mean?"

"You were genuinely flustered when the cute blonde waitress showed up. Something I should know?"

Derek slumped back in his chair and waved away her insinuation. "No. It's nothing like that. I only know her because I was a regular customer when I lived out this way. I was just surprised to see her still working here after all these years."

No sooner did he finish speaking than his gaze was drawn to a pulsing light over Kristy's shoulder. Across the restaurant, the front wall faded and rematerialized twice before it vanished, leaving in its place a black and green grid pattern from ceiling to floor.

"I love how easy it is to get you going." Kristy pushed her chair back. "So which way to the restrooms?"

"Uh, restrooms?" Derek's voice cracked as he shot forward in his seat.

"Yeah, I assume they have those here."

The wood-paneled wall reappeared behind her. Dakota scurried by and gave him a thumbs up. Derek cleared his throat. "First right past the fireplace."

"Thanks." Kristy stood. "Oh, and don't go running off with *Dakota* while I'm gone."

"Stop it." Derek rolled his eyes while Judy Garland started in with "Have Yourself a Merry Little Christmas."

A moment later, Dakota returned with their drinks. "Well, that was awkward. Good recovery, though, that line about going home for Christmas."

"Dakota, what happened to the usual waitress?"

"I altered your program. I thought it wise to step in and address these tech problems with you personally."

"Yeah, I read the note from management in my menu. Look, I don't want Kristy to know this is all virtual reality. Can you do anything for me?"

"The last thing we want to do is ruin your Christmas vacation, Mr. Marcus, but we just lost main power and had to switch to generator. The VR system is now running on UPS. The techs want to shut it down gracefully before—"

"How long?"

"Thirty minutes at most."

Derek sighed. "Then give us thirty minutes, please."

"I'll let the techs know. Of course, you'll be refunded the full cost of this session."

Derek shifted his gaze to Kristy as she approached the table. "Yeah, okay. Thanks."

He had downed his second beer before their food arrived.

Kristy draped her napkin over her lap. "Take it easy there, cowboy. Don't start pounding them down on an empty stomach."

"Sorry."

She frowned. "What's wrong? Having second thoughts?"

"What? No, not at all. Like I said before, I was just nervous leading up to the proposal." He cupped his hand over hers. "But now I can relax knowing we'll be together."

Kristy laced her fingers between his. "Forever."

The rumble of Derek's stomach sent them both giggling. "Sorry."

"Well, you know the old saying about the way to a man's—" Kristy jumped at a flash of green light outside the window. "Did you see that?"

Damn it, Dakota. You said thirty minutes! Derek shrugged. "I'm sure it's just a glitch with their holiday lights."

"No, I caught it out of the corner of my eye." She leaned close to the window. "It was like a huge grid."

When it happened again, Kristy spun in her seat and looked at the other patrons, all of whom were calmly eating or conversing, oblivious to the spectacle. "How could they not have seen that, and where's the waitstaff?"

"Kristy, relax. It's probably nothing."

In unison, ceiling and floor abruptly vanished. The walls soon followed along with every table except their own. Kristy gasped as the interior of the restaurant dissolved, leaving the couple sitting in silence, surrounded by a black and green grid.

"Probably nothing? Derek, what the hell's happening? Where are we?"

"In a holochamber." Derek slumped back in his seat and tossed his fork on the table. "I'm sorry, Kristy. None of it was real. Not the country house, not the mountains, not the lake. This is all virtual reality."

Kristy held up her left hand. "What about this ring? Is this fake, too?"

"No." Derek shook his head. "It wasn't fake. I loved you so much." He reached for her hand. "I always will."

"Why are you speak—" Kristy's form undulated before momentarily flickering out. She returned as nothing more than a distorted, pixelated mass. "—past tense?"

"Because you're not real either, not anymore. This day *did* happen four years ago, but now it's just a digitized memory."

With that, the illusion that had once been Derek's fiancée disappeared. He slumped over the table, cradling his head in his hands.

Across the holochamber, the doors parted to admit a tense and solemn Dakota, now donning the standard formfitting uniform of her employer, Virtually Real. "Mr. Marcus, please accept our apologies for the technical difficulties during your session. Two of our UPS batteries failed, forcing us to power down sooner than expected. You're more than welcome to return later this week and restart your Christmas simulation free of charge."

"It's all right." Derek rubbed his eyes and stared at the empty seat across from him. "In fact, it's probably for the best. There are no do-overs in real life and after four years, this façade has... lost its appeal."

"I'm sorry, Mr. Marcus. Please allow me to—"

"Derek. Call me Derek. We've known each other long enough. After all, you helped me recreate one of the happiest days of my life. You know how she died. You know my weakness... you know my pain."

Dakota nibbled on her lower lip before drawing in a sharp breath. "Management has also authorized me to issue you five VR sessions at twenty-five percent off with no date restrictions or expiration. You may use them anytime."

Derek was silent as he ran a finger along the edge of a table that would only remain solid until he moved away from it. "You know, every time I come here, I get so excited to see her again, even for just a few hours. Yet, I always leave here feeling like shit. I don't know why I keep torturing myself like this."

No sooner did he rise from his seat than it vanished along with the table. "Tell your management I appreciate the offers, Dakota, but I'm done hiding inside technology in a pathetic attempt to recreate a lost love at half off the regular price. No coupons will bring Kristy back. I'm sorry, I know I'm making this awkward. I won't waste any more of your time. Thanks for your help, Dakota. You did a fantastic job." Derek started toward the doors. "Oh, and Happy Holidays."

"Derek, wait. What about a New Year's Eve party?"

With a laugh, he shook his head. "You're persistent, I'll give you that."

"No, I mean a *real* New Year's Eve party with live human beings. At Jolene's Pub in the Theatre District, Upper West Side. Some of my co-workers and I are going. You're more than welcome to join us."

Derek folded his arms. "I thought employees weren't allowed to fraternize with the customers."

"And I thought you weren't coming back." Dakota ambled closer. "Look, I'm not asking you on a date, especially after all you've been through, but you said that I know your pain. Well, when I told you I was alone for the holidays, I didn't make that up. I work here every Christmas because I don't have anyone to share it with. You think you're pathetic for coming back here every year, but when I see you with a virtual rendition of your fiancée—one that I created—I envy you because that's more than I have. So, you tell me who's more pathetic."

"I'm sorry, Dakota. I honestly didn't know."

She shrugged. "Never too late to make up for lost time. New year, new start, and no strings attached, I promise."

"Thanks for the invite. I'll think about it." With that, Derek stepped through the doors into the corridor.

"I never knew the real Kristy," Dakota called after him, "but I doubt she'd want to see you isolate yourself, especially this time of year."

Derek stopped and lowered his head with a sigh. After a moment, he turned. "No strings attached."

"You have my word, but keep in mind it's a limited time offer, expires December 31st."

"Then I guess I should act now while supplies last?" He smiled in spite of himself. "You were right about Kristy, but wrong about being pathetic." With that, he sauntered off with a wave. "See you on the Upper West Side!"

CRANBERRY RIVER

Lorraine Donohue Bonzelet

The ocean waves rushed relentlessly over the water-soaked boulders which held steadfast through the attacks. I stood mesmerized by the frothy collision between land and sea. A powerful, yet serene, presence. The deserted carefree beach was a stark contrast to the crowded chaos that accompanied the Christmas season, especially with Melody's family.

Melody and I had been college roommates. Our personalities were similar despite our upbringing, though our Christmas traditions were vastly different. On Christmas Eve, Mom and I would gather with her church group for cookies and karaoke. Then on Christmas day, after celebrating at mass, we'd toss ham and sweet potatoes in the oven, open a few carefully chosen presents and binge-watch sappy old movies in our new matching pajamas. Melody's mom, Carol, had pity in her eyes when I talked about the simplicity. After Mom passed, Carol insisted that I share in their exuberant holiday celebration. *Celebration* is not the term I'd use, but it's been ten years and inexplicably I still attend.

Last Christmas, I sat on the boulders mindfully preparing myself for what I knew would be an exhausting evening. Then I navigated the sandy path to Carol's coastal cottage. In the front yard, I was greeted by an over-sized blow-up Santa rebelling against its rope restraints. Santa, with his cherub cheery grin, weaved and bobbed in the wind. When I opened the front door, the smell of cinnamon-scented pinecones filled my nostrils. Blaring Christmas music pounded my ears. Green garland, gold balls and twinkling white lights draped the doorways and banisters. Resin snowmen, reindeer, gingerbread houses and candy dishes decorated every flat surface. The clutter that normally occupied the living room had been replaced with presents meticulously stacked along the walls and under the Christmas tree. Wrapped in every patterned paper imaginable, the presents were decorated with color coordinated bows, nametags and swirly ribbons. I maneuvered between the folding chairs to strategically balance my gifts without smashing the bows or causing an avalanche. Relief.

As I made my way through the hall to the kitchen, Melody's family erupted with joyful greetings. Carol embraced me in a hug and reprimanded me for being late. "You almost missed dinner!" She returned her focus to orchestrating nine helpers, all relatives, in the meal preparation. She critiqued the thickness of the maple-sugar glazed ham slices and warned Melody's brother to cut slowly. "Haste makes waste!" Carol pointed to the pot on the stove. "Broccoli's boiling! It's going to be limp!" Then she yelled at the gabbing salad preparers, "Don't waste my water! I have to pay for that!" Melody glanced at me and mouthed, "I'm glad you're here," and continued to beat the heck out of the mashed potatoes.

After the food was devoured and stomachs bloated, the nieces and nephews chanted, "Presents! Presents!" which started the stampede... vying for the best seat...

deciphering names on glittery tags... passing presents over heads... ravenously ripping boxes exclaiming "ooohs" and "aaahs" and "thank-yous." I remained in the kitchen to pile the dirty dishes in the sink. I wiped the kitchen table clean in preparation for my gift that I'd hoped would bring Carol joy. By the time I'd reached the living room, everyone was up to their knees in shredded papers and bows. I joined the unwrapping frenzy.

The craziness slowed. Sweaters, socks, scarves, gloves, gift cards, and tchotchkes were haphazardly strewn about. Stillness settled in. Everyone sat silently as Carol opened her gifts: perfumed soaps, dish towels, tree ornaments and money. Money was the traditional gift to help her pay down her Christmas debt.

My green glittery gift bag was placed on her lap. With excited apprehension, she lifted the crimson crepe paper. She pulled out the white tablecloth hand-painted with dozens of red winking lobsters wearing Santa hats. "It's adorable! I love it!" Tablecloth in hand, she raced to the kitchen stubbing her toe on a box in the hallway. As she winced away the pain, she gave a crisp snap of the tablecloth, sending the other end soaring in the air. It gently floated down covering the spotless table. She smoothed the creases and draped the corners neatly over the sides. She made sure the tablecloth hung just right and admired the lobsters winking at her. Carol returned to the living room with a smile of approval. Melody flashed me a thumbs up.

Exhausted and overstimulated, the holiday adrenaline rush subsided. It was replaced by Carol worrying that someone was going to recklessly throw away expensive gift cards or perfectly good bows hidden between crumpled wrapping paper. As if on cue, Carol's annual lecture took center stage. She reminded us that today's generation is a throw-away, wasteful society and we'd all grown too persnickety and privileged for our own good. I was happy that the lecture was short. Carol finished by professing the sentiments she'd expressed for the past ten years, "Do you realize the time it takes me to shop and wrap? Yet, within minutes it's over! Next year we're having a simple Christmas." I couldn't help but smile at the thought.

Apple, cherry, pecan and coconut cream pies lined the kitchen table. Coffee, tea and a variety of juices occupied the adjacent kitchen counter. The post-lecture gloom gave way to giggles. I slid a hunk of cherry pie onto a holiday dessert plate, covering up the words 'Be Merry.' As I reached across the table for the whipped cream, merriness vanished. My elbow caught the rim of an unmanned cup of cranberry juice, spilling out a sea of red. The winking lobsters slurped up the liquid. The once snow-white tablecloth became a never-ending cranberry-stained river.

Carol's expression said it all! She mumbled almost inaudibly, "Why do these things always happen to me? Why can't I enjoy new things? Is that too much to ask?"

Instantly, my apologies and suggestions gushed... cold water... soap... I'll buy another one... My unheard voice sank deep within. Carol was not accepting solutions. Time stood still, everyone frozen in place. Carol tried to hold back the tears escaping down her face. Melody gave me a sympathetic look. I sensed everyone's underlying relief that this year's meltdown was not caused by them. I silently made my annual promise not to return next year.

The next hour passed slowly with nervous small talk, recalling happy memories, trying to lighten the mood.

Everyone picked at their dessert. Finally, goodbyes. Warm wishes. Hugs. Carol reminded me to drive safely. I acknowledged her request.

Six months have passed. I've asked Carol to meet with me so I can share good news – and talk about Christmas. I approach the house knowing that the dark window coverings are used to hide the clutter and disarray. As I enter the foyer, I see that the dusty Christmas decorations are still in place. The deflated Santa is lying lifeless on top of a mound of plastic shopping bags filled with irresistible must-have bargains. Carol is upstairs, promising to be down in a minute. I enter the kitchen, confronted by red winking lobsters still adorning their Santa hats. New stains are speckled about the tablecloth. What remains of the cranberry stain is so faint that the untrained eye wouldn't see it; a pinkish tinge that I'm not sure is even there. A reminder of a mere mishap that surged up a lifetime of disappointments for Carol.

Carol and I sit on a bench and watch the ocean waves pummel the boulders. Hours pass as Carol repeats memories I've heard many times before. Penniless... wearing torn and worn-out hand-me-downs... living in a village overwrought with poverty... a lifetime of living without... a lifetime of wanting... a lifetime of people ruining her things... Much like the cranberry river, her words spill unrestrained.

My shoulders tense and my jaw muscles tighten. I don't think Carol's comments are meant to hurt me, yet I feel the need to defend myself. I start to explain but she seamlessly keeps talking. The cranberry-stained tablecloth has been added to her long list of heartbroken stories. I realize that now is not the time to rebut her memories. She wouldn't hear me. I know that perception is a delicate dance – the timing must be right and both parties must be willing to listen.

Carol and I traverse the path back to the cottage. The sound of the ocean fades behind us. In front of us, I'm in awe of the sunset — ribbons of fiery oranges and vibrant yellows across the sky. I say a prayer of gratitude for nature's gifts.

I glance at my ring, excited about starting my family and my traditions. I'm certain that Carol hasn't noticed the diamond. She grabs my arm to steady herself on the sand and reminds me that she's getting older by the minute. Any day could be her last. In an instant, her mood shifts as she proudly announces that she's already started shopping for Christmas. She says she's glad I'm part of their Christmas tradition.

I need to tell her it's a tradition that I cannot keep. I will tell her... but not today.

THE CHRISTMAS ANGEL

MaryAlice Meli

Claire Allen folded the email she'd just printed, kissed it and tucked it into her sweater pocket.

She raised her window, her hands reaching up on each side of the frame and closed her eyes letting her face absorb the winter sun's pale warmth. She breathed a long sigh. It was going to be a great Christmas this year.

She smiled down her building's three flights. People of all ages lined both sides of the street to watch the annual parade that signaled the start of the Christmas holiday season. Scanning the puffy, brightly colored ski jackets, the real and fake fur coats along the small town's main street, one figure stood out. Claire's smile faltered as she focused on an old woman in a threadbare gray wool coat and matching cloche hunched slightly over a cane. Claire had seen her somewhere before.

The old woman stopped to watch the spectators, some of whom had already positioned their folding lawn chairs at the curb. She looked around her for a place to sit and settled herself in the sun on a low, concrete wall above the river. She wedged her cane between the wall and her leg and watched others strolling the main street admiring Christmas decorations in shop windows, buying small bags of roasted chestnuts or large, soft pretzels and huddling over creamy cocoa from mugs steaming in the frosty air.

Claire watched the old woman who, as the sun grew warmer, unbuttoned her coat, which Claire remembered as black the first time she saw her, not gray. A strengthening river breeze ruffled her long, ornament-free dress. She loosened the black scarf covering her white hair and re-knotted it around her neck, then replaced the cloche. Claire's faded blue eyes studied the old woman who, oblivious to Claire's scrutiny, scanned the passersby occasionally nodding.

Claire remembered where she had seen this woman before. It was last week in the doctor's waiting room, before her final tests. The old woman's appearance seemed more defined then, clearer. Claire couldn't put her finger on the exact difference. She appeared to be wearing the same clothing but now the coat, the dress, the hat, seemed lighter in color or maybe the woman had just changed her black coat to another of the same style in gray. Or maybe Claire's location looking down on the woman contributed to the difference. Claire shrugged, silly thoughts.

A sudden wind shift tugged at the cloche. The old woman lifted her arm to secure it but that sudden movement, viewed from Claire's perspective above, appeared as though the old woman was waving at her. Claire involuntarily stepped back behind the frame of the window, her heartbeat thundering in her chest. She closed her eyes, pressing her back against the frame, and deliberately slowed her breathing. Her hand brushed against her pocket and the crackling of the paper with the email renewed the thrill of relief and comfort it had brought her.

She turned to the window again to see her grandson, a husky young man wearing a wide, tartan scarf, standing in front of the old woman, his back to her. He was passing out fistfuls of wrapped Christmas hard candies from the town's Chamber of Commerce to the spectators, adults and children. He ignored the old woman as though he didn't even see her. Claire frowned. That was completely unlike Michael. He wrapped his scarf securely around his neck and moved on.

Bass drums and snares began a marching beat at the far end of the main street as trumpets and other brass instruments belted out Christmas carol melodies. The strollers now drifted to fill the few empty gaps on both sides of the roadway as the parade came closer.

More people also jammed the windows on the top floors of Claire's white-washed building. Marchers dressed in red or green or royal blue with gold trim strutted gracefully, tossing and catching their batons. Band members proudly lifted their instruments performing choreographed movements together to the rhythm of the drumbeats. Floats filled with tableaus slowly moved by with local teens as Joseph, Mary holding a live baby as Jesus, the three kings, angels and shepherds sponsored by various town organizations. Shiny convertibles from a local auto dealership carrying the waving parade marshal, the mayor, council members, police chief, and fire chief drove by followed by fire engines from a half dozen fire companies from towns nearby.

Watchers waved at the happy procession below except for Claire. She pulled on a puffy blue paisley jacket as she studied her contemporary seated along the wall. A blue tam covered her curly white hair and she watched as the other woman tucked the ends of her scarf inside her coat seemingly unaware of anyone's notice, used to feeling invisible. Claire closed her window and zipped her jacket. The other woman scanned the windows and stopped to acknowledge Claire. She nodded to her and lifted her hand in a gentle wave then pushed herself up on her cane and slowly continued her journey. Claire wanted to talk with her.

She disappeared from the upper window, reappearing at the doorway below, leaning on her own cane. She followed the other woman's progress hesitantly at first, keeping to the opposite side of the street. She had no trouble following her, their pace so alike, they could have been twins with similar debilitating maladies though Claire noted the old woman's coat seemed an even lighter gray. Old, she thought to herself with a silent snort, we're probably the same age.

Claire wore large sunglasses, blue ski pants, and high-top yellow sneakers her grandson had bought her for Christmas last year. The two women arrived at parade's end at the town's small cathedral in the main square. Though so close to each other now at the bottom of the church's shallow steps, Claire had trouble seeing the old woman who seemed not so much brighter now as faded or blurred. Claire's sunglasses were unable to stem the sun's glare and, as she squinted to see the old woman, all she could discern was the woman's nodding at her and her hand waving.

Michael came out of the parade crowd and put his arm around Claire's waist.

"Hey, Granny, are you going to church to pray for your sins or mine?"

Claire ignored his teasing and pointed to the disappearing figure of the old woman.

"Do you remember seeing that woman?"

"What woman, Gran? There's just a bunch of kids jumping around."

"It's the old woman you skipped when you were giving out candy."

"Gran, you know how much I love old ladies, especially cute ones." He gave her waist a squeeze, gently pulling her closer to him. "I'd never ignore an old lady. Sorry if that's the way it looked."

"Don't you see that woman up there with the cane?" she insisted, pointing with her own cane.

He squinted then shrugged. "Maybe I should wear sunglasses like you. The sun's glare is too much. I just see people from the parade going for hot dogs."

"Okay. Want to come to church with me? I'm not going to stay long, just to say a little prayer."

They started up the steps.

"Mom and Dad said you went for tests yesterday. Did you get the results?"

"I did," she said smiling broadly. She unzipped her jacket and pulled the email out of her sweater pocket and handed it to him.

Claire squealed and laughed as her grandson lifted and swung her around.

"Aww, Granny, I'm so glad. The tests results say your cancer is gone. Mom and Dad will be over the moon. I'm going to text them that Granny beat the Angel of Death."

He carried her into the church and set her down at the altar railing.

"This calls for lighting a bunch of candles," he said and shoveled a handful of coins and dollars into the bin under the rack of flickering votive candles and began lighting those still dark.

Angel of Death indeed, Claire thought. *She looked just like me although I'd never wear a cloche. But it did add to the non-scary effect. And that's a good thing, helpful, not to be afraid of death. Will I feel this way if the cancer comes back? Hmmm. If I see that old woman again, maybe I'll go through my wardrobe and pick out something updated, something more colorful.*

Claire smiled and began to chuckle. *The Angel of Death gets a makeover and a name change— just for the holidays.*

A GIFT

Lori M. Jones

"Joe, maybe we should pull over," MaryAnn said, gripping the handle of her car door.

I think she may have said it twice before, but her words had jumbled beneath the sound of the flapping, angry wipers. It was as if we'd driven right under a waterfall, our remaining day's light blotted out by menacing clouds and endless water. I was driving by pure faith and the guidance of an occasional flicker of red brake lights in front of me. The smell of the fresh banana nut muffins she'd baked for our trip still hung in the air.

Our nerves were a bit rattled and perhaps this trip was bad timing. We were supposed to be heading to a relaxing night away, a date night, before my job interview tomorrow. The position of Statistics Professor—my dream job—had opened up at Messiah College.

"Joe!"

"Mary, I think I'm okay." I kept forging on, determined to get to our destination to make my wife happy, and accomplish our goal of an enjoyable evening.

I needed to take her mind off the fact that we'd suffered our fourth miscarriage a week before. And to distract her from the disappointment that we wouldn't be telling our families happy news next week on Christmas

Day, I'd booked us a room at the nicest hotel near the university and made reservations at the finest restaurant.

MaryAnn's sadness had been overwhelming and I was desperate to ease it. Of course, I was sad too, but my grief couldn't compare. She'd carried the babies inside of her. I had loved the idea of them, but she was the one who had held them. And she held a guilt along with it because her body, as she'd say, was the reason we couldn't have a family. Her chances of getting pregnant were slim, and now it seemed her ability to carry a child, the doctor told us, nearly impossible. Immediately after leaving the doctor's that day, she filled out the paperwork to begin the adoption process, yet she said it didn't feel right. *"Maybe God just doesn't want us to be parents, Joe,"* she had said through sobs that night.

"Holy... I've never seen rain like this. And in December."

I couldn't see the hood of the car let alone the pavement, but I stubbornly kept driving.

Cars were scattered along the side of road, reminders of what a fool I was being. The rain began to lighten but a new tinkling sound on the windshield alarmed us.

"It's starting to freeze," MaryAnn said.

"Damn."

I lightly pumped the brakes to see if I had traction but the car swerved out of my control. Black ice.

"Damn," I repeated, then mercifully, our tires caught again.

"Pull over," she said in a calm, but demanding voice.

I did. There was no one else on the side of the road along this stretch. A couple other cars passed us slowly. And then it was quiet except for the sound of the rain intensifying again and transitioning into ice.

"So how long do we wait here?" MaryAnn asked, staring ahead as evening faded into night.

"I don't know. Maybe until we see a salt truck?"

The thermometer on my dashboard showed the temperature had fallen to thirty-two degrees.

"Sir! Open your window!"

As if I needed more adrenaline coursing through my body, a man's face appeared to my left and his loud tapping made me almost jump through the roof. The police officer's nose was nearly touching the glass. "Josh Brady" his nametag read. I opened my window as fast as my finger could push the button.

His full beard was dripping and crusting over in ice. "There's a car over the hill. Do you have a phone? Can you help? I totaled my car on my way to the station. Phone and radio are busted."

He pointed over toward the woods and I could see the front of his car smashed against a tree. I noticed a small cut on his forehead, and he dabbed it with the back of his hand.

"I have no service," MaryAnn said, pressing her thumbs all over her screen.

"The car is that way, past mine. There's a woman unconscious in the driver's seat."

I popped my door open and followed the crusty-bearded officer into a ravine, slipping the whole way. Mary was behind me. "Mary, stay in the car."

"No, I'm coming."

I wasn't surprised except, perhaps, that she wasn't ahead of me.

We got to the car and she ran to the passenger side where the window was broken. Without hesitation, her arm was inside the window unlocking the door.

"Mary! The car is sliding. Get out of the way!"

She jumped into the passenger seat. The car handle slipped from my hand and the car slid further into the ravine, but onto more level ground. Now probably stuck for good in the mud.

My fearless wife reached over the woman's big pregnant belly and opened the driver side door.

"She's bleeding bad from her head, but she has a pulse."

"Hello, miss, can you hear me? We are here to help you and your baby. Please open your eyes!" Even though MaryAnn was a teacher, she sounded like a trained EMT. But, then again, it was a job that probably contained some of the same field experience.

"I'm heading back to the road to get us help," said Officer Brady. "Stay with her. There's a rag in the backseat you can use for her wound."

I pressed the rag into her gash. She moaned, so I said again, "Please open your eyes. We are here to help you. You've been in an accident."

And magically, she opened them. Her eyes locked with mine and her pupils looked large and eerily bright black. "My water. My water broke. This isn't my baby."

There was no time to try to decipher what that meant.

MaryAnn mumbled, "Oh, my God," while reaching between the air bag and the woman's stomach, apparently searching for some lever or button to push her seat back.

I found the plastic handle before she did and yanked on it, making the seat fall backwards. My wife was still talking to the woman, who was no longer responsive.

Just then, I heard a clamoring up on the hill. Ambulances and police cars were at the officer's wrecked vehicle and perhaps other cars that were stopped. They must not see us. I tried to gain my footing in the challenging terrain.

"Hey! Down here!" My voice sounded so small, and I feared they couldn't hear me or see us. I ran toward them, but then I heard my wife's pleas.

"Don't leave us. Don't leave us."

The woman was awake again, but apparently from my wife's words, not alert. MaryAnn held the woman's hand and said, "Sarah, stay awake, stay with me. You're going to be a mama. You're going to want to witness this!"

Apparently, the woman's name was Sarah.

"Thank you. For saving my life. And the baby's. But I'm not gonna be a mama."

And she closed her eyes. "Sarah, Sarah!" my wife yelled. Sarah looked so young to me now, like a child asleep.

Sarah moaned and her eyes opened again. She cried out. MaryAnn grabbed onto her one knee, and terrified, I took the other. My wife slid the woman's dress up, and I instinctively looked away, but I could see out of the corner of my eye that my wife was going to work. The light from her iPhone's flashlight was illuminating the intimate scene.

Sarah screamed out again and pulled her head toward her knees.

"I see your baby's head!" MaryAnn yelled.

And the yelling and the pushing continued. Then MaryAnn pulled a bloody baby from between the woman's legs, guiding it around the steering wheel.

"Oh my Lord. It's a boy."

I took the long white rag we'd used to stop Sarah's bleeding and opened it up to wrap around the baby. The boy was still attached to the umbilical cord and I had no idea what to do. I was in awe of my wife, who acted as if she'd done this before.

I ran again toward the first responders by the road and screamed with all of my might.

"Down there!" one of the EMTs yelled to the others.

With thick mud on my shoes, I hurried back to join my wife who was cradling the baby boy in her arms, wrapped inside the white rag.

One of the paramedics pushed past me as another entered the car from behind my wife.

I felt so dizzy I thought I was about to faint. Within seconds, I heard the baby's cries break through all of the chaos. What a beautiful sound.

Sarah was placed on a stretcher while my wife held the baby, now wrapped in a clean white sheet. MaryAnn looked at me and said, "Sarah doesn't want to hold the baby." Her eyebrows pressed toward each other in a look of dismay.

The rain had stopped and we both stood beside Sarah's gurney after MaryAnn asked the paramedics to stop for a moment.

My wife and Sarah held hands. The baby boy was asleep in my wife's other arm.

"The baby's adoptive family just backed out," Sarah explained in a rush of words. "I was on my way from seeing them. The mother found out she is now pregnant with twins and the father's job was relocating them overseas. I was distraught. My water broke. Then the rain hit and I must've blacked out, but I don't remember." She was breathing like she was in labor again. "I just don't know what I'm going to do now."

We were then asked to step aside and Sarah's gurney was loaded into the back of the ambulance. Without permission, my wife, still holding the baby, went with her.

I grabbed the arm of one of the EMTs and asked, "Can I join them... please?"

He hesitated and said, "I'll ride up front since no one is in any medical need."

A different paramedic joined us and we were all shut inside together. The lights were so bright, and I could now see my wife's shirt was covered in blood. The ambulance jolted forward, taking off toward the hospital.

MaryAnn leaned closer to Sarah. "I'm so sorry the family backed out. But are you sure you want to give this baby away? We can't have children, I can't carry a child, and this is such a beautiful gift."

"I'm only eighteen. My parents want me to go to college. I don't want him." She burst into tears. The baby whimpered too. "Would you take him, MaryAnn? We can do an independent adoption. Please. You can't have children and he needs parents."

The look on my wife's face was a mix of a relief and joy I hadn't ever seen before. It was the joy I'd wanted to see on my wife's face for years.

MaryAnn looked at me. "Joseph. She wants us to adopt him." Her words were breathy and slow.

"Oh, Mary... Yes, let's do it. We can do this. But can we?"

Sarah's cries were now cries of relief and joy and my wife was now in tears.

"Please. Please adopt him. You were meant to be here tonight. You saved us. I can pick who he goes to, and you two... you two. I mean it's almost Christmas... and your names. Mary and Joseph? Is this even for real?"

The paramedic interrupted us. "And, you do know what town we are in, don't you?"

I shook my head.

"Bethlehem, Pennsylvania, folks," he said.

We gasped and laughed, and MaryAnn wiped tears from her eyes while staring down with love at the tiny baby... wrapped in swaddling clothes.

A fear of seeing my wife completely disappointed again smacked me. "Sarah, are you sure? Please... this is serious. Are you absolutely certain?"

"I've never been so sure of anything. You both are my heroes."

MaryAnn rubbed Sarah's arm as tears streamed down her cheeks. "Sarah, we would've never found you had it not been for the officer who pointed us toward you. Officer Josh Brady is the real hero."

The paramedic stopped taking Sarah's blood pressure and popped his face up, his eyes bulging from his head. "What? When did you talk to Josh Brady?"

I explained how he told us where Sarah was and asked us to help.

"Um, Joshua Brady was killed in a car accident tonight. We had just finished pulling him from his mangled car when we heard your calls for help."

Everyone's face went pale. My wife's mouth hung open. She managed to say, "But we saw him. His head was bleeding and he took us to Sarah."

"That's impossible, ma'am. He never left that car. He died instantly."

My wife and I looked at each other. I could tell she probably wasn't breathing. All of my mathematical skills could not make this add up.

Sarah could barely speak, choking on sobs. "Was that his ghost? His spirit? An... angel?"

Everyone just shook their heads slowly, eyes wide with disbelief, trying to absorb it all. No one said a word as we pulled into the driveway in front of the hospital.

We never left Sarah's side and we took turns holding her hand until her parents arrived.

And one week later, we were able to share happy news with our family on Christmas Day.

We got to introduce our son to our family. Our sweet baby boy, our precious gift, Joshua Brady.

STARS OF PEACE

N. J. Hammer

Kix Koleman stared at the two-foot artificial evergreen for so long that the white star at the top blurred. The multicolored branches blinked hypnotically. He closed his eyes and waited for the afterimage to fade from behind his eyelids.

The Christmas decoration was ancient. Almost three hundred years ago his great-great-great grandmother had cherished it, then willed the thing down through the generations. His mother had forced it on him after his most recent visit home.

Always tenacious, often scary, his maternal parent was a mighty power all her own. He agreed to take it just to get her off his back. But why he'd brought it with him on this voyage was a mystery, even though it was the proper season for the accessory. Maybe, deep down, he knew he'd need some of his mother's persistence.

Her words ran through his mind. *"Never quit negotiating until the problem is solved, until the situation is settled to everyone's satisfaction."* Arbitration had been her gift. And her legacy to him. Or perhaps it was a curse. Sometimes he wasn't sure which.

The Hotites, Karmasins and Placimits had been fighting for nearly as long as his tree had existed. Now their societies were nearly eradicated, their planet,

Setsitima, just short of decimated. Each group claimed its way was the only right way. Its gods the only true gods. Their heavens welcomed only those that believed the same as they did. All others were sinners needing to be converted or eliminated. And each had spent centuries trying to conquer or destroy the others, either covertly or in active warfare, until there was nothing left but ideology.

This summit was likely their last chance.

The leaders had asked Uni-Star Trust, the Hata Family's organization, to arbitrate what everyone hoped would become a solution, a last ditch effort to save these societies from extinction.

Kix had been assigned the task. He opened his eyes and watched the tree blink at him.

Earth had been like this alien world once. It had matured, reached a place of peace. Had acknowledged that civilized peoples could have differences but still live in harmony without trying to force their own ideas and rules of conduct on each other. They might not agree, but they were no longer trying to kill each other.

Kix stared at the tree. Maybe that's what the groups needed. A symbol, something outside of themselves, something that didn't belong solely to one society. But what? The star on top of the tree blurred again.

Maybe.

He grabbed his e-pad and left his quarters, heading straight toward the small observation deck located topside of Rand MacGregor's starship *PaxVobiscum*. Uni-Star Trust might be the money behind this arbitration effort, but everyone knew who the captain of this vessel was. And who would make the decision to stay or leave. He often wondered what MacGregor had done to deserve that type of sponsorship.

Kix had been on the starship twice before. He admired how MacGregor handled the danger when prior negotiations failed abruptly... and violently. The captain's quick thinking and superior piloting saved the lives of everyone onboard. Kix would be forever grateful. Rand had since become a good friend, something Kix admittedly could use more of.

When he'd been asked by Uni-Star to conduct these negotiations, he'd specifically requested *PaxVobiscum* as a condition to taking on the assignment. There was something special about Rand MacGregor, something almost mystical. Kix intended to find out what it was before this voyage ended.

The starship was equipped with all the newest bells and whistles. Especially impressive was an observation deck that made view-ports look like pinholes. While on-station orbiting a planet, the screens covering the O-deck's clear plexisteel dome were withdrawn and the scene from real-space—sunshine or dark sky—was visible to the observer. They were night-side of Setsitima so the legions of stars surrounding the planet were in plain view, as was this world's triple moons.

Three. There had always been something special about that number, even among Earth's ancient peoples. Maybe he could use that to his advantage. Three main societies on the planet, three moons circling in balance, and maybe, if he could locate and relate three stars in close formation, he could find an element of agreement.

Points of light.

He pulled up a star chart, searching for the closest, brightest stars that each faction could see. It didn't matter what names the tribes had given them. It didn't matter how far away or what type of stars they were. The only thing that mattered was that they were close together and of the same magnitude. A trio of bright lights existing in harmony.

This planet's inhabitants had journeyed through the stars at one time. But when one group gave up space travel, they all did, fearing one would take over while the others were not on home world. Now they all watched the sky for signs and portents.

He could use that. If he could find the right stars, in the right places. An added blessing would be if they were at exactly the same declination over each of the groups' territories. Which was actually likely since the planet's livable land masses centered around the equator. Each tribe should be able to see the trio once every day, in Setsitima's case, every fifteen Earth-hours.

A point of recognition.

It didn't take long to find what he wanted. They formed a nearly perfect triangle, a good sign. He searched for names the groups might have given the stars and was surprised to find that they had the same meanings when translated from the individual languages. That indicated the monikers had to have been chosen by tribal ancestors before the groups had separated, long before warfare had begun. Another good omen.

He sat down and leaned against the back of a bench positioned at the edge of the small garden that occupied most of O-deck. The air was heavy with the smell of the multicolored flowers he could see all around him. A stone path snaked through the short trees and bushes planted around the base of the transparent dome. Kix wasn't surprised how very Earth-like the space felt. MacGregor was an Earther after all.

Home.

Perhaps he needed to add a touch of sentimentality to his negotiations. A sense of what the tribes' world had been like before they'd nearly destroyed it. And what it could be like again if they worked together. They would need to cooperate. They would need to honor their ancient peoples, their shared ancestry.

If he prepared an image-vid, the representatives could actually see what might happen as a result of their peaceful interaction. So they didn't have unreasonable expectations, he would also point out how hard it would be, how long it would take. But it could be done. With help.

A point of understanding.

Kix smiled. Uni-Star Trust might not like what he was going to propose. But Rand MacGregor would. And that was all Kix needed.

It only took ten hours for Kix to arbitrate the agreement. He watched with deep satisfaction as the leaders nodded to each other, clasping hands in accord. The treaty was a good one. He said a silent prayer that the resolutions each society had made would hold.

A point of reconciliation.

Two hours later, Kix watched MacGregor convince ZacAn Hata, the director of Uni-Star, to send the agreed upon assistance. He was also pleasantly surprised when Rand coaxed both him and ZacAn into acknowledging that he would make an excellent addition to the crew of *PaxVobiscum*.

Now Kix and Rand gazed at a tableau in Rand's quarters. The Christmas tree sat next to a pearl-white figure of an angel that had belonged to Rand's father. The two decorations complemented each other nicely.

Kix had to agree. And so did the two men seated side by side, enjoying a moment of well-deserved peace and quiet.

FATHERS AND DAUGHTERS

Jennifer Diamond

I organized the Christmas loot under the tree by folding my sweaters into their boxes. It created a bold display. In 1985, everything was bold, the reason I didn't belong. Before I threw the Nike box across the room, I set aside the unopened presents and admired how well I had wrapped a tiny ring box. That small gift represented a monumental wish. We would take those gifts to Gram's later in the day.

I flinched when the empty shoe box crashed on top of a pile of crumpled wrapping paper and looked at my Mom sleeping on the couch. Thank God she was still snoring. Dad continued to strum on his acoustic guitar but paused his Christmas hymn humming.

"Jennifer." He only called me 'Jennifer' when he teased me. When I'd angered him, it was 'Jennifer Dawn.'

"Don't you already have a pair of those?"

"No, these are pink."

They were exactly like my gray pair, but pink kept the mean middle school girls from telling me I had boys' shoes. I knew, before I unwrapped them, they were pink Nikes.

I knew what everyone in my family was getting for Christmas because I did all the wrapping, even my own.

My heart sang when the scissor blades sheared the long roll of paper with a sweet, prolonged *'sh'* and *'shup'* at the end. Sharp, creased corners and invisible tape added to my satisfaction. I coveted my sister's alt-rock cassettes when I wrapped them. I planned to copy them using Dad's new double tape deck before she went back to college.

I wrapped all the presents for our extended family, too. We pulled names at Thanksgiving and Mom got her Dad's. 'Paha' (what we called him) wished for a diamond ring. While explaining the story of her miserly grandfather, who wore a flashy diamond pinky ring, and how Paha had wanted it, Mom wiped at her eyes. Her tears broke my heart a little. She then beamed over the huge cubic-zirconia. It was a gaudy ring, and obviously fake, but I knew I shouldn't burst her bubble. Surprised when she gushed at how well I wrapped the black velvet box, I imagined Paha opening it. My chest felt warm and liquidy. Ever since she started working full-time, Mom mostly barked at me about our messy house. With not one harsh word during our wrap session, I was glowing like a Christmas Eve luminary.

After lacing my new Nikes on Christmas morning, I went to the kitchen for a grocery bag. The woodsy pine scent of our live blue-spruce smelled fresh again when I went back into the living room. I picked up wrapping paper and boxes. The bigger boxes required extra force to crush them flat into the thick brown paper bag.

"Don't put any plastic in there," Dad said. "I'll burn it later."

My fingernails scratched along the carpet as I scraped up the last bits of tissue paper. A blue-green pine needle stabbed straight under my fingernail. That's just perfect. This is my reward for cleaning up the place? I'm the only one picking up crap around here and this is the thanks I get? I wallowed as a red dot appeared under my nail. It bubbled and I knew it would eventually turn black.

"Careful."

No kidding. I didn't dare say it out loud, because there was nothing worse than disappointing my dad by acting disrespectful.

At my Gram and Paha's, the rigged doorbell buzzed like the game Operation. That's why I liked pressing it, even though we walked straight into the house.

Everyone pushed me through the three-foot-wide foyer before I took off my coat, leaving me sweaty, holding bags of presents, while Gram hugged me. Her hugs had a comforting weight, like the heavy blankets she piled on top of me during sleepovers.

The uneven heat hit hottest in the kitchen, especially with the oven roasting a Christmas turkey. After hugs, Gram stepped onto the braided rug in front of the stove. She turned the knobs for the two front burners and struck a long kitchen match. The smell of sulfur mixed with natural gas transported me back ten years or more, when after a bath, Gram had wrapped me in a warm towel. I sat on her lap in front of the gas-fired space heater where the sapphire hues of the flickering flames mesmerized me. Those smells, which many people find unpleasant, calmed my anxieties.

Paha yelled, "Here come the River Rats." I wasn't offended though, because it was a reference to our small riverfront town seven miles away. He sat in his favorite rocker/recliner. But the chair didn't rock or recline because it pressed against the pool table. The pool table was piled high with pieces of small appliances and engines. This was Paha's room, but my safe haven—a space in which we watched his game shows together. He would tease Gram, baiting her into arguing with him about whether the *Price Is Right* ladies had plastic surgery or not. He played hours and hours of Atari with me, letting me win most of the time. This was his laboratory, where I sat on a stool, watching as he created his inventions.

After dinner we all sat in the living room, waiting for someone to start our Secret Santa exchange. With a small family, I guessed who bought my gift by the process of elimination. Aunt Deb gave me nail polish. A full sixteen years younger than my Mom, Debbie was gorgeous and vivacious. She made anyone she talked to feel like the most important person in the world. Debbie demanded a squeezing hug as thank you. She immediately started painting my nails. Receiving a manicure from Debbie was extra Christmassy.

"No. No. No."

My mother's voice pierced the contented chatter. Deb quit painting my nails.

"Where is it?"

Her pitch spiked my blood pressure. She picked up bags and tossed aside wrapping paper.

"I can't find Dad's present."

Debbie set the nail polish on the coffee table. Everyone rushed to Mom's aide, but I shied away from the mayhem. I knew what was missing. I knew she couldn't find the tiny jewelry box I wrapped the night before.

"Jenn brought them in, didn't she? Where'd you put them? Did you put all of the presents in the bags?"

The peppered questions felt like accusations. My chest tightened. Christmas dinner churned.

With the mad hunt finished, Mom sat in tears, paper crumpled in her fists. Dad knelt beside her and whispered.

"Jenn," he then said, "we're going to go get it."

I stifled eye-rolls and followed him out to the car. Deb wasn't done painting my nails. Why did I have to go? Why couldn't my sister? She stayed for Gram's chocolate cake with from-scratch peanut butter icing.

I opened the back door to the white sedan.

"What are you doing? Get in front."

For the first time, I sat in the front seat with Dad driving. It was somehow different than when Mom drove me around. The view enchanted me, like I was special, like I was as special as my older sister, who sat there many times before I ever did. He reached into the inside pocket of his jacket and pulled out a pack of Marlboros. Then he stuck an unlit cigarette between his lips and pushed the auto lighter. When little, I thought my dad was the Marlboro Man. I thought it was him in all of those magazine ads.

"Don't tell your mother."

The red glow of the hot coil sizzled when it lit paper and tobacco with a familiar *tss* I hadn't heard in months. The smell took me to the back seat of the car on long drives. Dad cracked his window to draw out the smoke no matter how cold it was outside. At night, I twisted my body to watch the orange sparks bounce off the black pavement, thinking it looked like fireworks.

"You know why this ring means so much, right?"

Yeah, Mom told me the story last night when I wrapped the damn thing. Only half-listening to my dad, I studied my smudged nails. Trying to smooth out the imperfections only creased my fingerprints into the polish.

"You know what a cheap son-of-a-bitch your great grandfather was?"

His curse snapped my attention.

"That man owned a bunch of coal companies, but his kids lived like paupers. Did you know your Great Aunt Mary was thirteen when their parents left them alone for almost a year? You're thirteen now, right? Imagine taking care of six little brothers and sisters all by yourself."

I didn't really like babysitting. Not because I didn't like kids, but because all the worst-case-scenarios fueled my anxiety, if only for a few hours. I couldn't picture a whole year.

"Two of them were still in diapers. He was wealthy, but such a miser. And nobody knows where the money went. Your Paha had such a hard life. What he witnessed in the war? You know where he was stationed, right? You know what shell shock is?"

The rhetorical questions sucked the air from the car. I shifted in my seat and looked at Dad. Had I ever really looked at him before? He squinted at the gray sky, creasing his wrinkles deeper than when he smiled. His bushy eyebrows hung low, creating an illusion of sternness.

He cleared his throat and took a deep drag on his cigarette. My breaths stuttered. My eyes stung. I didn't want to know any more, but I couldn't stop listening. A tiny puff of smoke drifted from his mouth as he continued.

"Your Paha always talks about a diamond his dad wore. That man walked around wearing fancy clothes and jewelry while his kids went hungry."

It hit me. This was the real story, not the PG version

Mom told. I felt older, like he trusted me to understand the harsh truth.

Another puff of smoke pulled away from his head and thinned to a white line, like it wanted to escape. A wind gust bullied its way into the car, swirling the smoke into a curlicue. It darted into the back seat, an apparition.

"It was horrible. It wouldn't happen in today's world. Those kids should never have been left alone. Unbelievable."

He took a last drag and flicked the butt out the window. If it had been night, I couldn't have resisted the urge to look back at the fireworks.

He put his hand inside his jacket again and the plastic sleeve crinkled, but his hand came out empty. He used his thumb to spin his college class ring on his right ring finger. The gold was dinged, the blue stone chipped, and the words 'Penn State' were worn smooth, but I never saw Dad without it.

"His dad was wealthy and powerful but gave nothing. Your Paha spoiled his girls. They've never had much money, but he gives everything."

He scratched at his early afternoon stubble, inhaled and let it out long and slow.

"Do you think, if he only had his dad's diamond ring, then his whole life would be different?"

The question lingered like the cigarette smoke still hanging in the air.

"He does."

We tore apart my neat Christmas gift display. We split, looking in all the other rooms. I looked in the most unlikely places because our house seemed to swallow things. It hid needed items among the stacks of newspapers behind the couch, or slipped important documents within the piles of my mother's *Psychology Today* magazines. The thieving troll seemed to live behind the stereo. When searching for coins, cash or car keys, I looked there first. I pulled the speakers off the cabinet, but came up empty. After I put the speakers back, I walked into the kitchen where Dad searched.

"Keep looking."

I stretched, and through the haze of a head rush, I noticed a reflection of light. The light bounced off a wire basket. The basket held folded brown paper grocery bags.

"Where's the bag with the Christmas crap I cleaned up this morning?"

"I burned it before we left."

He turned and went out the back door. I met him at the rear edge of our yard where the burn barrel sat on cinder blocks. He stirred the contents of the barrel with a broken shovel handle.

"This isn't working."

He lifted his cowboy boot and pushed the side of the barrel. It crashed into the wet grass, breaking apart into bits, with a plume of soot mushrooming. The sky descended and the clouds broke open. Freezing rain tamped the black dust, turning the contents of the burn barrel strewn around us into thick tar. He poked aside half-burned newspapers and I caught a glimpse of the date from three years ago.

I shivered, permed hair stuck to my forehead, my jacket heavy with rain and glasses fogged from my breath.

"You're going to have to dig."

"Huh?"

"Push aside the big stuff."

I moved a bit of old newspaper by its burnt edge.

"No. Really get in there."

He threw the stick, bent over the pile across from me, and dug his hands into the muck. I pulled up the cuffed sleeves of my coat and stuck my fingers into the guck, centimeter by centimeter. It was cold and gross, slimy but chunky at the same time. Brown blades of grass poked through the black mess.

My heart clenched. It was my fault Paha would never get his very own diamond ring. I pictured my grandfather a toddler, still in diapers. His little legs running to the door when his parents came home after an entire year. He reaches to grab his daddy's hand, the hand where the pinky ring sparkled. But his dad doesn't pay any attention. His dad turns away from him. He can't catch a glimpse of his father's face. The shine of the pinky ring is all he can remember. All he ever wanted was that diamond.

My hands moved with more purpose. I scooped a softball-sized glob in the palm of my right hand and dripped the goo onto the ground. I chose a different pile and did the same. Nothing. I pushed my hand into another pile to scoop, and found a solid chunk the size of a lump of coal. One year, when Paha worked at the strip mine, he gave us each a lump of coal for Christmas.

My breath sucked in and I couldn't exhale. Dad stopped mid-shovel, his bushy eyebrow raised at one corner.

"Holy cow," he said, like a real cowboy.

The velvet covering was burned raw, smothered in gritty ashes. I held the box away from my body, like a grenade without its pin, certain the cheap knock-off ring was a molten blob. I'd ruined Paha's special gift.

"Open it," Dad said.

My eyes stayed glued to it when he plucked the box from my hand and cracked it open. Spots blurred my vision. Fat raindrops switched over to swirling snowflakes. Shoulder to shoulder, we inspected it while the snowfall whitened the burned slough around our feet.

"Wow," was all I could manage.

The melted satin lining had cooled to a crust. The fire had charred the princess-cut cubic zirconia black. The fake gold band was gray and warped, but still intact. The ring was in one piece, if not unblemished.

We left the mess in the yard and stomped the snow off our shoes before going back into the house. At the bathroom sink, I eavesdropped while Dad called. The plan was for me to wrap the box again.

"Yeah, she threw it away with the wrapping paper," he said with an amused tone.

A pain stabbed my chest sharper than the blue-spruce pine needle under my fingernail. He only said the truth, so why did it hurt? Wasn't I the one cleaning the house? Wasn't I the one who wrapped all of the presents in the first place? Wasn't I the one who found it in the garbage?

Black ashes smeared my face. It reminded me of when my English teacher explained the purpose of William Blake's poem, *The Chimney Sweeper*:

When my mother died I was very young,
And my father sold me while yet my tongue
Could scarcely cry 'weep! 'weep! 'weep! 'weep!
So your chimneys I sweep, and in soot I sleep.

With the water on, I leaned close to the mirror, waiting for it to warm. I looked like a chimney sweep, covered in soot. Rubbing my hands under the freezing water only drove the inky crud deeper into my fingerprints. It reminded me of getting booked and sent to prison. What crime had I committed? I only wanted to help, but somehow it was all my fault. If I hadn't helped in the first place, then I'd still be at my Gram's instead of digging through the ashes of our Christmas morning trash.

I grabbed the golden bar of soap off the countertop and dug my nails into its slimy surface. I scratched at my palms under the now, finally, warm water, but the tar-like substance was stubborn. The nail polish peeled off in strips. I took off my glasses and scrubbed my face. My selfish thoughts burned my cheeks.

On the drive back to Gram's, a memory flashed. After working a midnight shift on the dragline, my Paha had walked into the kitchen covered in coal dust. Was it irony that he'd dug in the dirt for a coal company when his very own father had owned several? And, was it irony when coal, exposed to enough time and pressure, transformed into diamonds? He deserved better.

Dad took out his last cigarette and squeezed the empty pack into a tight ball. From the passenger side mirror, I watched the final sparks bounce off the dark road. They looked far away, distant miniatures of the fireworks I remembered.

We gathered around Paha's rocker/recliner, where he sat like a king. Dad held the gift like it was the state championship trophy, then passed it to Mom.

"Hey, Dad," she said, "you remember what you wanted for Christmas?"

"Hell, no. I can't remember what I had for dinner."

Paha held court. Gram smiled wide though she hid her gapped teeth for every photograph. My sister and Aunt Deb looked like twins sitting next to each other on the couch, with matching beaming faces. Dad winked at me. I turned lighter than air, like the fizz escaping a freshly opened can of Coca-Cola.

Dad said, "The Christmas present that made it through the fire and back. Open it," using his best radio voice.

Always the showman, Paha shook the tiny box. "What could it be?" he asked.

"It's your only Christmas wish," Mom said.

He took his time peeling off the bow and each piece of tape. He removed the paper all in one piece and set it on his lap, the plain white backing face up and red Christmas tree print face down.

"Would you take a look?"

When he opened the lid, black ashes rained onto the white underside of the gift wrap. They were like the negative burn photo effect of snow falling into a strip mine pit.

"My very own diamond. How did you know?"

"Oh, Dad." Mom had her hands pressed together, fingertips peaked in front of her mouth, like a child saying grace.

Paha slid the blackened ring on his right pinky and held his hand high.

"Get over here, River Rat."

I stood beside his chair and took his hand in mine. His fingernails had black grease under them, embedded evidence of his latest invention. He pulled me into a side hug and I leaned into him, resting my face on top of his soft head. His white hairs clung to my cheek for a second. I wiped the wetness away, smoothing his hair flat.

My great grandfather may have had a flashy diamond ring and loads of money, but Paha had a charred fake. It may have been a cheap knock-off, but it was everything. It was the gem that bonded fathers and daughters.

THE DAY THE MAGIC DIED

James Robinson, Jr.

As a child, I'll never forget the excitement, the sheer joy I felt as I ran to the tree on Christmas morning. The anticipation was tangible—you could cut it with a dull kitchen blade. Perhaps you know the feeling, it was the culmination of the centuries-old Christmas magic—reindeer on the roof; bells jingling; the conclusion of the Christmas list; and, of course, Santa, Mr. HO! HO! HO! himself, coming with toys for all the good little boys and girls—a ritual for all times.

One morning is etched forever in my mind. I was eight years old and living in Wichita, Kansas. As I jumped from my bed and ran to the living room, I could see the shadow of a new bicycle under the tree. My heart leapt from my chest. I don't recall being as thrilled since.

Ah, yes, Wichita in 1961. One cold winter day, I swear I saw a tumbleweed sweeping down an alley behind my home. Okay, maybe not. One movie theater in the whole town. God knows I needed a jump from the Christmas action once a year.

Those were the days; I was a few years removed from a seat on the Big Man's lap. In the early days, I told Santa what I wanted. My mother stood within shouting distance and smiled as he barked out my request for loot. As we all know, it was a ruse. She already knew what I wanted. Santa just reinforced the con. My mother was the intermediary, the conduit, the go between.

Money was tight. My father was a minister and a poor one at that. I got a bike and that was it—no Solo Beats headphones, no cell phone, no laptop, no $100 worth of gift cards to cash in at my favorite retail spot. I didn't go searching for our Verizon Cable passcode to get wireless connectivity. For god's sake, we barely had electricity. Do I sound like an old curmudgeon? Like some killjoy who talks about how they had to walk twenty miles to school and come home for lunch? Well, shake my hand and call me "James, Jr." I guess that's what I am.

I was ten, yes ten years old, when I found out the awful truth. I slept in on Christmas morning the year after the end of the fairy-tale, after the defrocking of Santa. I opened adult presents in unadorned boredom like every other schlep—socks, shirts, underwear, and cologne.

The loss of Christmas sleight of hand wasn't a total surprise. My friends had been eating away at the miracle for a year or two. The little urchins. "Don't you know your parents buy your toys?" one of the little cretins said. The first time I heard the disparaging comments I did a '60's version of "talk to the hand." Their words went in one ear, marinated in my immature little brain for an instant, then came battered, mangled, and dog-eared out the other. But they kept it up, those worldly friends of mine. Then, slowly but surely, maturity stepped in and began to guide me toward the truth.

"Okay," I finally asked my mother at the decade mark. "Is there a Santa or not?"

I mean, this was a dream that she had orchestrated for half a decade—the reindeer dancing on the roof, the milk and cookies charade, the Santa knows if you're sleeping or awake bit, naughty or nice—I listened for the red-suited-one flying Caribou on the roof and we didn't even have a chimney. Such was my faith in this travesty.

"No," my mother said with sadness in her eyes, "there's not."

I can't say that I was all that shocked.

"What about the cookies and milk we left?" I said looking for clarity.

"See that man over there?" She pointed to my father. "He ate them."

It was all coming together, now. I looked at my father with no evil intent at that moment, but although I couldn't spell the evil or comprehend it at the time, he was complicit. He will forever be known as an accomplice, one of the infidels who dragged me kicking and screaming from innocence to adulthood. Thanks, Dad, I thought we was boys.

For her part, my mother, for all her cries of innocence, may as well have signed me to a contract, a notarized document she had tucked away for just such an occasion.

After digging through a safety deposit box containing her marriage license and last will and testament, she would have pulled out my official document of post-Santa lifelong, work slavery and said, "Here, sign on the line. An X will do. This statement acknowledges that you know the truth and have officially stepped into the world of adulthood. When you turn sixteen, I'll help you with a resume and you can enter the workforce. We'll have to get this validated. Congratulations, son, now let's go make a batch of cookies."

I know, I'm lucky in a way. I'm a Christian. There are religions who never live the magic. And in my youthful insouciance, I never thought about the hard, cold facts of it all. At sixty-seven years of age, I'm aware of the physics involved. My tainted heart knows that to achieve the speeds necessary to reach every believing soul in the world, Santa's sleigh would burst into flames. I realize that the big fella had no way of knowing what was in your heart and didn't have enough room in that sack and on the tiny sleigh for sufficient toys to cover every devotee on my street let alone the whole world. As a cynical, feisty, almost septuagenarian, I would now say, "Yeah, Santa's elves could make all those toys as North Pole non-union labor—when pigs fly." Problem is, those dumbass reindeer were themselves flying.

But none of that matters; I lived the dream. So, what if my friends took a sharp stick to my bubble and my father ate the snacks meant for my mythical Christmas hero. The dream had to end sometime. I mean, nothing lasts forever. I'm being too kind—you back-stabbing bastards.

Junior and senior high school, puberty, needless erections, proms, a driver's license, and college all waited in the wings. I jumped the broom in 1976, fathered three beautiful daughters—daughters who have gifted me with six energetic grandchildren. Most of all, I had to become a real-live Christian—learn the true meaning of Christmas. Santa is still in the game, but not the Santa I knew. These days, he's a big-time commercial sell out. For shame, Santa. We know what you are.

But I'm still not keen on forgiving the messengers. Absolve me for carrying a grudge for low these many years, but there's a special suite in the hot place for people who foster a sham, perpetuate a dream and then unceremoniously take it away; or friends you consider your wingmen in a fantasy, who discover the truth and rub it all in your innocent little face like a shaving-cream pie.

Life went on after the hoax, but it was never quite the same. Damn you. Damn you all. You fakes, philanderers, and prevaricators. Parents, you meant well, but you took me into the land of the zombie working class. My backstabbing, little eight-year-old friends, you proved the adage that misery loves company. All of you were there when that truth willed out, when a little boy lost his enchanted virginity. The day the magic died.

Okay, so that was a nice, warm ending to a smart-aleck essay. Maybe I shouldn't characterize it as such, but I tell it the way it is. Beat me with an aluminum bat—it's the way I roll. You would think that having this ultimate fraud perpetrated upon me—up until this age anyway—by those closest to me would cause me to inform my children right from the get-go about a December 25th visit to Santa Suckerville.

You might figure that the notion of the red-suited, obese one being a sham, comparable to a one-day social call from that slippery—yeah, right, sure, there's a Bigfoot; I saw that 1965 tape—would give me cause to stop the madness. Surely, Sasquatch would scarf down some of my wife's chocolate chip cookies. But, no, quite the contrary. The trauma of losing the mojo didn't stop me from continuing the tradition with my own three girls.

Did passing on this act of sedition make me a hypocrite? Probably. But frankly, my wife and I—she seemed to move on seamlessly from her Christmas experience—didn't want them to miss out on the fun. And surely, we could tone down the—sorry, there ain't no Santa—ending a bit and leave them without the scarring.

So, we went for Christmas bigtime. Take, for instance,

the Cabbage Patch Dolls frenzy. Cabbage Patch Dolls weren't the kind of dolls that you walked into a store and casually picked up off the shelf like the ageless Ken and Barbie. Cabbage Patch Dolls in their infancy—with their big round heads and long rope-like braids—were a craze like no other and our girls had to have them. Each doll came with its own birth certificate. Even at my age, thirty-years removed from the Cabbage Patch fury, I can still remember the names of my girls' dolls. Don't believe me? Well, there was: Jaime Minnie, Yolanda Eleanor, and Kirkwood Franklin. So there.

Once we realized that the dolls were a frantic commodity, and that procuring them was going to take some resourcefulness, my wife began calling around to toy stores to find out if they had any in stock. Ha, ha, silly girl. Soon, she reduced herself to asking the brokers what day truck shipments of the precious dolls were being delivered—a lot of work for the, now exposed, Kris Kringle to get the credit. But get the credit he did. Santa still got the kudos, we still didn't have a chimney, and I was now eating the cookies.

But the magic didn't die for my girls by our hand; it was a matter of good detective work. My wife wrote letters from Santa and the Easter Bunny and the girls deduced that their mother's handwriting looked suspiciously like the two phonies. They were more mature and sophisticated than their old man—living in a more sophisticated world. We had to fess up. The magic of Santa and the Easter Rabbit had died in one fell swoop and my three beautiful ladies went on as if nothing had happened.

And we were the better for it. We started a new tradition of having dinner on Christmas Eve and a big breakfast in the morning. Later we all went to the movies on Christmas day, came home, and enjoyed leftovers. Life is good. No more fantasy; the truth prevails. The King is dead. Long live the King.

SHAPING CHRISTMAS

Denise Weaver

I love everything about Christmas—the thrill of little children's anticipation, reverent strains of Silent Night, and joyous celebration with family and friends. The mesmerizing glow of lights, a chill in the air, bells ringing, and the aroma of warm spiced cookies all evoke a sense of home, love, and the joy of Christmas. Memories flood in, lists are made and crossed off, excitement is in the air.

Several women shaped my view and approach to the season. My exquisitely artistic mother was skilled at decorating our home, and she loved turning our Christmas tree into a work of art, making it a showpiece and her most important task. Her gift-wrapping was a close second as she tenderly crafted bows and placed them just so on each meticulously enveloped and color-coordinated package.

Christmas Day was always quiet, with just my parents, brother, and me. However, the week between Christmas and New Year's Day was a fun-filled time with visiting grandparents and aunts and cousins, "seeing what Santa brought" each year, excited *oohs* and *aahs* replacing the more subdued tones. There were cookies and pies, candy canes and chocolate-covered cherries, hot chocolate and eggnog.

As much as I wanted to—and still wish to have her ability—I could never begin to mimic my mother's style and panache. She was adept at color coordination, the proper placement of scented candles, the right textures to include. Lacking her talent, I chose minimalism instead, both for the big holiday and throughout the year.

Other women helped me develop a different focus than that of my mother. I loved my Aunt Vi dearly and wanted to emulate her adroitness with food that she lovingly created. Her preparations seemed effortless and I witnessed the joy her aromatic and delicious edibles delivered. But more than the food, it was the love and acceptance that she stirred into each dish. I later used her as an example in teaching my children to give of themselves.

It was at the suggestion of my fourth-grade teacher, Mrs. Hay, that I asked my parents to take me to church. That was when I found the true meaning, and the reason for, this very special holiday we call Christmas. I'm still easily brought to tears of gratitude for her gentle guidance in my pursuit of what has been nearly a lifelong faith journey, along with a deep affinity for listening to and singing sacred music. What a wonderful gift she gave to me!

My mother-in-law was a sweet, unassuming woman, who stressed fairness and doted on her children and grandchildren. Going to her house at Christmas meant lots and lots of cookies. To access the living room, everyone had to pass through her steamy kitchen where, on Christmas Day, countertops were lined with trays of cookies. The usual suspects: black & white cheesecake bars, sand tarts, sugar cookies, lemon bars, and chocolate chip cookies.

One of the most anticipated and exciting preludes to Christmas morning is setting out cookies for Santa. Some families also leave carrots or special cookies for the reindeer, too. In my household both as a child and an adult, chocolate chip cookies with their chewy yet crisp texture and just the right amount of sweetness were deemed to be Santa's favorite.

My favorite early elementary teachers, Mrs. Dull and Mrs. Hay, instilled a love of learning, and even today I enjoy researching topics. It is thought that the tradition of leaving cookies and milk for Santa Claus became entrenched in the United States during the 1930s as a result of the Great Depression. Parents wanted their children to learn the importance of giving to others and sharing, and that they should be thankful for the gifts they were fortunate enough to receive during those difficult times.

Ancient Norse mythology is credited as the original source of this tradition. The god Odin was believed to have an eight-legged horse; children would put out food for the horse hoping that Odin would stop, allow his horse to eat, and would then leave gifts for the children in appreciation.

Today, the custom takes various forms throughout the world. In Denmark, children still believe that horses lead Santa's sleigh, so they leave crunchy carrots and sweet hay. Swedish children set out a creamy rice porridge. In Great Britain and Australia, the selection is a savory-sweet mince pie. And, I guess it's not surprising that my Irish kin include a pint of Guinness along with their cookies to quench hard-working Santa's thirst.

Here in the States, milk and cookies remain a favorite traditional thank you to Santa. Christmas cookies, of course, are ubiquitous in most areas, and the list of varieties is expansive. There are plain and simple shortbreads, homey peanut butter blossoms, and beautiful but time-consuming elaborately decorated cookies that grace many holiday trays. Flavors can range from the very mild sand tart to an intense spicy-hot ginger cookie.

The whole process of cookie baking evokes many pleasures for me: reliving the memories of baking with my kids when they were young, absorbing the scents and textures of combining and baking the ingredients, experiencing the joy of sharing the tasty treats with friends, family, and people I may not even know.

As my kids were growing up, I tried to make Christmas a fun and enjoyable time, while still focusing on the birth of Christ and what that means to us. We spent hours making cookies and handmade ornaments, crafting gifts for their grandparents and teachers, singing carols and reading Christmas stories.

I've recently adapted my holiday cookie baking tradition to one of baking with several good friends. We make a full day of it, starting in the morning, taking a break for lunch, and finishing just before dinner, producing hundreds of cookies in a variety of shapes, sizes, and flavors. We bake in my kitchen, contributing ingredients and baking tools, making old standards like shaped and decorated sugar cookies and chocolate chips as well as introducing family favorites the others have not had such as Neiman Marcus cookies.

As we bake, we talk, laugh, and sometimes cry, sharing important details of our lives and all the while bolstering our friendship. Amid the enticing aromas, the clang of baking sheets, and the heat of multiple ovens, we talk of family, health concerns, losses, and memories; we disclose tragic moments and let each other in on hilarious incidents. At the end of our marathon baking session, cookies are divvied up between us, plus a large container is designated for our church's annual children's musical.

I miss my mother's beautiful decorated trees, my mother-in-law's lovely Christmas dinner and cookies, and baking with the kids. But as demonstrated by the recent tradition of baking with good friends, there are always new opportunities and adventures waiting to be discovered that can shape one's view—just like the revelation of Christ's birth, death, and resurrection gifted to me by a loving teacher.

I'm sharing one of my mother-in-law's recipes, a family favorite and easy to make. May you experience joy and love as you prepare and share your talents, whatever form they take, and employ all your senses as you enjoy this wonderful holiday season. Merry Christmas, and don't forget Santa's milk and cookies, maybe even an Irish pint, plus some carrots for the reindeer!

Blanche Weaver's Easy
Black & White Cheesecake Bars

1 (12 oz.) pkg. semi-sweet chocolate chips
1/2 cup butter
2 cups graham cracker crumbs
1 (8 oz.) pkg. cream cheese
1 (14 oz.) can sweetened condensed milk
1 egg
1 tsp. vanilla

1. Preheat oven to 325 degrees.
2. In medium saucepan over low heat, melt chocolate chips and butter, stirring until smooth. Remove from heat.
3. Stir in graham cracker crumbs. Reserve 1/4 cup mixture for topping. Press the remaining mixture in 9x13-inch baking pan.
4. In large bowl, beat cream cheese with electric mixer until smooth. Gradually beat in sweetened condensed milk, then egg and vanilla.
5. Pour over prepared crust. Sprinkle with 1/4 cup reserved crumb mixture.
6. Bake until set, 25 to 30 minutes. Cool. Refrigerate about 2 hours. Cut into squares. Yield: 35 squares. Refrigerate leftover cookies.

BUON NATALE

Cara Reinard

Buon Natale to everyone
Nona's table is set for twenty-one
Nearly forty will show, that's for sure
Va bene, always room for one more

The house is twinkling with lights and laughter
Dogs bark, children scamper
Missy said she was done the year before
Tonight her stomach is swollen, smile pure

No vino for her as the drinks are poured
Crystal glasses clink, hearts soar
Red and white and amaretto on their lips
The uncles say, *Ah Missy, you can have-a-sip*

The feast occurs the night before
Apps and dishes and sweets galore
Just no meat tonight, pretty please
Ignore the sopressata—it goes with the cheese

Heads are bowed, a prayer is said
The baby cries, the cousins chirp—*Amen*
Wedding soup is ladled, grated parmesan a must
Thoughts are offered to those no longer with us

Dinner is spread, no less than seven fish
How much baccala can you fit on your dish?
The mussels go fast, simmered in a garlic-butter melt
Nobody eats the smelts

Bellies are full, but the aunts brought treats
Cookies are unraveled from plastic sheets
Vanilla in the air from pizzelles and iced Christmas trees
Uncle Tony will fight you for the last cannoli

Presents abound under the tree, open one tonight
Tomorrow—the other three
We celebrate, but are reminded of the true meaning of
seasons past
And if we're lucky, we might even make it to midnight
mass

FIRST NATIVITY

Larry Schardt

I always wanted to live the life of Grizzly Adams (without the bears, of course).

I had just begun my new job in the Appalachian Mountains of central Pennsylvania, 200 miles away from my childhood home in Pittsburgh. I was excited to start as district conservationist in Mifflin County.

The first morning coffee chat was the time for me to get to know the staff. When Gerry heard I was living in a hotel a few blocks away she left the group in a hurry.

Minutes later, she came back shaking with excitement. "Larry! Your worries are over!" She couldn't hold in the news any longer and interrupted Donna's story about her dog. "I just spoke with my husband. We own a small cabin that is available to rent. Sounds like it would be perfect for a Grizzly Adams kind of guy. My husband's name is Skip." She handed me a small piece of paper with his phone number.

"Thanks, I'll call him on my lunch break. This is awesome," I said with a smile as big as Yogi's.

I sat at my desk, did some paperwork, and waited until lunch. At the age of twenty-nine, I felt like it was about time to move into a house. Noon could not have come soon enough.

I made the call and, without knowing it at the time, in a few hours, I'd be walking into my dream pad. As I turned the corner and drove down a long narrow mountain road, I could see the porch. I knew at that moment the cottage was mine.

Skip was leaning over pulling weeds at the end of the road when he saw me. It happened so fast. I was in awe. He began babbling about how much the rent was and about the electricity when I stopped him with, "I'll take it!"

The next day I rushed to the office. "Looks like I'll be moving! Skip showed me the cabin last night. It's way out in the middle of nowhere. Out in Havice Valley... It's perfect. Just in time for the Christmas season. It'll be my first Christmas away from my family. I need to make this special. Thanks again," I said and gave Gerry a hug.

Christmas has always been something special... The fragrance of pine, balsam, and cinnamon... Finding the perfect gift for those special people... Glitter, tinsel, sparkling lights... Cheer and goodwill... Smiles on every face! The holidays are a sacred time of year, blessed with traditions, magic, and life lessons.

One of my favorite memories was putting out the family nativity display. It contained a wooden half barn with straw glued on the roof and floor. The figurines were molded from clay, with robes painted bright colors and faces shaded and lined to give a realistic appearance. It was a treasure in every way.

As the oldest of nine, I had the honor of making sure Jesus was placed perfectly in the manger after it was set up under the tree.

Our family would begin shopping the day after Thanksgiving. I always told myself that when I moved out and was on my own, one of my dreams was to carry on those wonderful holiday traditions that make life rock and kindle memories of family and youth. This was the holiday to carry on those traditions in my own place.

My tiny log home fulfilled my back-to-nature dreams. It was my first home after getting out of college. As life went on, I graduated from sharing rooms... to apartment living... to living in a half-a-double... Now, at last, a home of my own. Not just any home. My dream cabin far out in the wilds.

Excited to celebrate Christmas in the woods, I cherished the idea of starting my heirloom collection of holiday decorations. Most essential was the manger.

I was prepared for a fairytale holiday in my new surroundings... The snow, lights on the outside bushes, the decorated Christmas tree, and the smell of the embers in the fireplace...

To make the scene complete, I needed to find that perfect nativity. I searched far and deep. I combed the department stores. No luck. I explored antique shops. No luck. I tried craft shows. Still no luck. My choices dwindled. My hopes diminished.

One afternoon, my friend Judy came to check out my new place. "Wow! Nice job! Looks great," she said.

"Thanks, Jude! It's me, for sure. I am trying to make it feel like home but I'm not having any luck finding a manger," I sighed.

"What about Englishtown? Have you ever been there? It's in Jersey." She talked nonstop. "They have a huge flea market! I know you'll find something there." Her ever-present smile glowed and her voice radiated with excitement as if we were going on a treasure hunt. "Let's go on Saturday!"

"Sure. It's certainly worth a try," I said. "It'll be a great chance to get some of my other shopping done, too."

"It's about a four-hour drive. We'll make a day of it," she said.

That Saturday I felt like I was going on a school field trip. On a bright and shiny December morning, we hopped into the car and made the trek to Englishtown.

By the time we got there, the parking lot was packed. We parked amidst the thousands of cars, then walked for what seemed like miles. We wandered for hours checking out display after display. I found lots of Christmas gifts, but still no nativity.

I gave up. Disheartened, deflated, and defeated, we decided to leave.

Just as we were about to turn and head back toward the car, I spotted a nativity set up on top of a box on one of the last vendor's tables. I ran over.

I carefully examined each intricate figurine. Mary, Joseph, Jesus in his crib, three shepherds, three wise men, sheep, cows, and an angel...

All colorful... All beautiful... All perfect!

"How much do you want for this?" I asked the guy behind the table.

"Ten dollars," he said. That was a lot back in 1983.

"Ten dollars?" I answered. "Wow! Why so much?"

"It's a one-of-a-kind, hand-painted set. I found it in my mother's attic. You won't find anything like it anywhere," the kindhearted gray-haired grandfatherly merchant explained.

"Well, it's exactly what I've been looking for," I admitted. "Alright, I'll take it."

I slipped my hand into my pocket and pulled out my last folded bill. Pleased with our find, Judy and I made our way back through the parking lot.

As soon as I put the nativity into the trunk I turned to Judy. "Yeah!" We high-fived, close the car door, and bragged about our bargain for the four-hour drive home.

We felt like little kids.

Once there, I honored each character with its own special spot. Knowing the history of the set made it so much more special. The setting was the magnificent final touch that made the cabin shine with a Christmas glow.

Later that week, Judy asked, "Do you want to go back to Englishtown? I still have a lot of shopping to do. Saturday okay?"

"I just got paid. Are you trying to get me to spend all my money already?" I asked. "This time you buy breakfast and I'm in," I teased.

The weekend came and another fun day was ahead. We hurried off on a new adventure.

We wandered around the flea market buying more gifts for the people on our lists. When we walked by the merchant who sold me the one-of-a-kind nativity I stopped in my tracks. Judy crashed into my back.

There, sitting on his table, were three more one-of-a-kind nativity sets, exactly like mine. I realized I'd been duped. We burst out laughing.

I thought about my mom's favorite saying, "The best things in life aren't things." The nativity was a thing...

In a few short years the paint chipped, the colors faded, and the figures crumbled.

But... that merchant gave me a gift far more important than 'a thing.' He gave me a lifetime of chuckles and a holiday memory to last forever.

'TWAS A HARD DAY'S NIGHT
AND ANOTHER AULD LANG SYNE

Sherren Elias Pensiero

B eing a drummer with a classic rock band was never on my Bucket List, but I did get the chance to tour with the Beatles on New Year's Eve, 2009. Now before you start to think that I can see dead people or that senility is not too far off, let me clarify that my magical mystery tour was made possible through the cultural phenomenon known as the Wii Rock Band game—the premier Christmas gift that year.

Rock Band was an edgy way to experience music on the Xbox or PlayStation 3. Players could simulate a concert by using controllers shaped like musical instruments, and by watching virtual portrayals of the Beatles performing forty-five songs from their history. The fun part was that gamers could create their own band and seek global rock stardom while learning to master guitar, bass, drums and vocals. *"Play it loud. Live the ultimate music experience on the highest-rated rhythm game to date,"* touted the Wii ads that coerced my niece to splurge on this mega-entertainment as a surprise for her daughters.

The surprise was on me as I was invited to their home for a New Year's Eve bash and asked to join my great nieces (ages eight and ten) for a jam session. I was in shock that they were still enthralled with their Rock Band gift a whole week after Christmas!

"Aunt Sher, Aunt Sher, come be a Beatle! We know you love them! Do you know how to play Nintendo?"

"Of course!" I wanted to seem cool. "I've been playing it since Lisa and Tara gave us the Wii Golf/Bowling/Tennis game last Christmas." Our daughters had the weird idea that the Wii would keep their dad from watching TV through his eyelids.

Truth is, neither of us remembered how to even start the game, so I was bluffing when I said I could play. But I figured I could wing it since I do play piano, and I know three guitar chords, and I have a mellow contralto voice like Karen Carpenter. I wish.

I figured wrong.

As I eyed the word-screen and the expansive peripherals—guitar, bass, drums, and microphone... what, no keyboard? I instinctively picked up the guitar. I'd learned guitar in college at the height of the folk music era, so it was a logical choice for me.

With guitar in hand, I assumed the stance. I propped my bionic knee onto the ottoman, placed the strap around my neck, and positioned my left-hand fingers on the red, yellow, blue, and green frets. I was ready to jam!

And a dead-ringer for Bonnie Raitt playing back-up for Lennon and McCartney.

"Wait, wait, we have to pick a song," my nieces bellowed. "Did you ever hear of 'Lucy in the Sky with Diamonds' or 'A Hard Day's Night'?" Did they think the Beatles were new?

"Right on! I pick 'A Hard Day's Night'." They insisted on 'Lucy'. Why ask?

We started the game, and being the talented, coordinated, and short-term memory deprived musician that I am, I couldn't remember which colored frets corresponded with which chords on the TV screen. By the time we got to the word "Diamonds," player two—that's me—crashed. I was thrown out of the game and blown a huge raspberry sound from the animated Fab Four. *PFFIITTHHPFFIITTHH!*

Dissed by George Harrison, The Quiet One!

"Let me try vocals this time," I whined. I picked up the microphone just as the words to "It's a Hard Day's Night" flashed across the screen. I was pompous enough to think I wouldn't need my reading glasses since I know the words to all the Beatles' songs by heart. Wrong again. I messed up just after "I been workin' like a dog."

PFFIITTHHPFFIITTHH! This time from Sir Paul McCartney.

Determined not to lose the game or my dignity, I sat down behind the only remaining instrument: the color-coded drum set. I've never had good eye-hand coordination, so I was certain I couldn't keep one eye on the screen, two hands going in opposite directions, and tap my foot at the same time. Is that multi-tasking?

But with sticks in hand, fear in my heart, foot on the pedal, and "Revolution" cued up on the screen, I was ready to Wipe Out!

I didn't miss a beat. My nieces were proud of their Auntie! And no raspberry from Ringo!

My tour with the Beatles was an awesome musical experience—not to mention a sweaty workout—to usher in the New Year. Even a virtual tour with them rocked my world throughout a hard day's night and into another auld lang syne.

Happy New Year from a wannabe rock "Starr."

CONTRIBUTORS

LORRAINE DONOHUE BONZELET, a retired engineer, has always been a picture book enthusiast at heart. She spends her free time analyzing picture books and writing stories. Her passion for writing is tied with her passion for travel; both of which she does whenever and wherever she can. She also enjoys running, kayaking, reading, and taking pictures of odd, interesting and unusual things. She resides in Maryland with her loving husband, two beautifully kind daughters, two tabby cats, and wildlife feasting on her vegetable garden.

JENNIFER DIAMOND holds teaching certificates for speech/language therapy and reading specialist and state licensure for speech/language pathologist. She also holds the national Certificate of Clinical Competence for Speech Language Pathology. She has worked as a speech therapist and substitute teacher in the public school system for over twenty years. Inspired by her students, she dreams of writing Hi-interest/Lo-readability fiction for teens who are reluctant readers, to encourage them to read independently for enjoyment. Her current work in progress, *How We Spin: A Novel,* won 3rd place for the 2019 Pennwriters Annual Contest, in the Novel Beginning category.

jenniferddiamondwriter.wordpress.com Facebook @Jennifer.D.Diamond.writer Instagram @jennifer_d_diamond_writer

WENDE DIKEC is the author of three young adult novels and seven adult books written under her pen name, ABIGAIL DRAKE. She adores snow, and secretly thinks getting trapped in a cozy cabin in the woods for a few months might not be so bad. After living abroad for many years, in places with very little snow, she finally settled in Beaver, Pennsylvania, with her husband, three sons, and a Labrador retriever named Capone. Capone does not share her love of things cold and wintery, and would prefer to live on a beach and drink rum punch.

PHIL GIUNTA's novels include the paranormal mysteries *Testing the Prisoner*, *By Your Side*, and *Like Mother, Like Daughters*. His short stories appear in such anthologies as *A Plague of Shadows*, *Beach Nights*, *Beach Pulp*, the ReDeus mythology series, and the Middle of Eternity speculative fiction series, which he created and edited for Firebringer Press. As a member of the Greater Lehigh Valley Writers Group, Phil also penned stories and essays for *Write Here, Write Now*, *The Write Connections*, and *Rewriting the Past*, three of the group's annual anthologies. He is currently working on a science fiction novel while plotting his triumphant escape from corporate America where he has been imprisoned for over twenty-five years.

www.philgiunta.com, Facebook: @writerphilgiunta, Twitter: @philgiunta71

KIMBERLY KURTH GRAY was born and raised in Baltimore where she finds daily inspiration for her writing. The winner of the William F. Deeck-Malice Domestic 2009 Grant for Unpublished Writers and a 2017 Hruska Fellowship, she is a member of Sisters in Crime, Guppies, and Pennwriters. Her short stories have been published in Cat and Mouse Press and Level Best Anthologies. In addition to working on a historical novel and writing short stories, she appears monthly as The Detective's Daughter on the Wicked Cozy Authors blog.

Science fiction has been N.J. HAMMER's favorite genre since childhood. For this author, crafting an intriguing story is as important as building the essence of a unique world. Masters of classic science fiction, such as Arthur C. Clark, Isaac Asimov, Ray Bradbury and Gene Roddenberry are as much her heroes as the most contemporary masters of the craft. In addition to writing science fiction for adults and middle grade readers, to pay the bills she's sold encyclopedias, worked in retail sales, added up the numbers as an accountant, clicked the computer keys as an administrative assistant and has driven the rambling roads as a real estate agent. But she always comes back to the story. njhammerauthor.com

HILARY HAUCK is a writer, translator and poet living in Pennsylvania. She has lived in three countries, hiked in the Himalayas, ridden a dromedary at sunrise in the Sahara, and watched bodies being burned on the banks of the River Ganges. Her travels greatly influence her writing, and she never tires of exploring the cultural and sensorial lenses through which people experience the world. A recent graduate of RULE XVI, Hilary is current president of Pennwriters, and co-founder of the Allegheny Regional Festival of Books. She gains immense inspiration from the Mindful Writers Retreats, and writes about mindfully finding #storyeverywhere at www.hilaryhauck.com.

EILEEN ENWRIGHT HODGETTS is working on the fifth book of her Arthurian saga, *Excalibur Rising*. She is also the scriptwriter on a soon to be released movie and author of a number of stage plays. She is a happy transplant from the United Kingdom to the United States by way of Africa and her travels are often reflected in her characters and the places where they can be found. She has attended every Mindful Writers Retreat so far and the company of other writers has changed her life and her writing forever. www.eileenenwrighthodgetts.com

LORI M. JONES is a freelance writer and an award-winning author of women's & children's fiction. Her first children's book, *Riley's Heart Machine*, was released in 2012 and was inspired by her own daughter's heart defect. *Confetti the Croc* followed in 2014 along with her debut novel, *Renaissance of the Heart,* which was awarded the silver medal by Readers' Favorites in women's fiction. Her second novel, *Late for Fate,* was released in 2016 and her first middle grade novel, *Freaky Heart,* is currently on submission. Lori is represented by literary agent Gina Panettieri of Talcott Notch. Lori sits on the national board of directors for The Children's Heart Foundation and is the president of the Pennsylvania Chapter. She enjoys traveling to schools to deliver assemblies on writing stories from the heart. She resides in her hometown of Pittsburgh with her husband, two daughters, dog and bunny. www.lorimjones.com

RAMONA DEFELICE LONG writes short fiction, creative nonfiction, personal essays, prose poetry, and is crossing over to novel writing. Her work has appeared in literary, regional, and juvenile publications, and she has received artist fellowships and grants from the Pennsylvania State Arts Council, the Delaware Division of the Arts, the Virginia Center for Creative Arts, the Mid-Atlantic Arts Foundation, and the SCBWI. Her short story "Voices" was nominated for a Pushcart Prize in 2017, and in 2015, her artist journey was selected by the National Endowment for the Arts to represent Delaware on the United States of Arts map. Ramona is a transplanted Southerner now living in Delaware. www.ramonadef.com.

JANET McCLINTOCK grew up in Sloatsburg, New York, a small town in the lovely Mid-Hudson Valley, where she rode motorcycles and horses and hiked in Harriman State Park. She joined the military and finally settled down in Pittsburgh, Pennsylvania. She is a member of International Thriller Writers, Professional Writers Group, and Pennwriters. In 2014 her first thriller, *Worst of All Evils,* was published by Black Opal Books, which became the first of the Iron Angel series, followed by *Hottest Places in Hell, The Only Sin,* and *Cowards Never Start*. She is currently working on a Christian fantasy and a Christian science fiction suspense.
janetmcclintock.com Twitter @Janet McClintock
Facebook @JanetMcClintockAuthor

MARYALICE MELI lives in Steelers/Pirates/Penguins country, aka Pittsburgh, PA, and has written nonfiction in past careers in education and journalism. She earned a master's degree in writing popular fiction at Seton Hill University. Now retired, she writes short and flash fiction, children's stories, middle-grade mysteries, and has begun reading all the books on her shelves designated *TBR when there's time*. She placed third in Pennwriters's 2014 short fiction contest and had two short stories published in Rehoboth Writers Guild anthologies. She's also been published online in Every Day Fiction, InfectiveINk, and Untied Shoelaces of the Mind.

AMY MORLEY is a former journalist turned reading specialist who spends her days surrounded by books, and her nights surrounded by Yorkshire terriers. Born and raised in the Steel City of Pittsburgh, Pennsylvania, Amy ventured north to settle in the rural outskirts of the small, albeit bubbly town, of Grove City. A published essayist, fiction enthusiast, and accomplished teacher, Amy's poem "The Hour Has Come" was published in the first Mindful Writer's Retreat Series Anthology, *Into the Woods*. She is concurrently working as a freelance editor, and writing a sweet romance Christmas novella inspired by her poem "Reminiscing on the Nostalgia of Happier Times."

If life imitates art, then SHERREN ELIAS PENSIERO's life mirrors the fictional Jessica Fletcher of "Murder, She Wrote" fame: English teacher, writer, busybody, amateur sleuth, busybody, college professor, busybody, widow, and bestselling author. Well, except for the bestselling author part. After thirty-one years as a high school Language Arts teacher, Sherrie took an early retirement to begin a second career as a writer. She founded The Write Solution, a home-based consulting firm that produced well-honed writing and editing solutions for companies and individuals. In addition to operating the business, she served as an adjunct writing professor at Allegany College of MD, and a work-for-hire writer/editor for several community agencies. Sherrie is the co-author of *Self-Esteem for Old Broad*s and the sole author of "The BROAD View" newspaper column. She is spending her second retirement developing her own writing style for the creative nonfiction genre.

CARA REINARD is an author of women's fiction and domestic suspense. *Pretty Dolls and Hand Grenades* and *Last Doll Standing* were published in 2016 through The Wild Rose Press. Cara is employed in the pharmaceutical industry and currently lives with her husband and two children in the Pittsburgh area.

JAMES ROBINSON, JR. hails from Pittsburgh, PA. He has written both fiction and non-fiction. His first book, *Fighting the Effects of Gravity: A Bittersweet Journey into Middle Life*, is a humorous look at midlife filled with autobiographical anecdotes. *Gravity* won an Indie Book Award. His fiction consists of a three-book series chronicling the life of The Johnson Family. Mr. Robinson's book, *Death of a Shrinking Violet,* consists of thirteen humorous essays.

Award winning author Dr. LARRY SCHARDT is known for his presentations on success, leadership, motivation, happiness, and living with a great attitude. His passions are teaching, music, the outdoors, and people. As a professor at Penn State University for twenty-six years, his students tagged him as the best and most fun. Larry also captures his audience when he is a keynote speaker at conferences and retreats. He posts a daily motivational blog on Facebook where he brightens his audience with the beauty and positives of life. He encourages everyone to live with gratitude, thrive with gusto, and explore the world with a sense of wonder. Larry loves sharing joy, kindness, and secrets of success in his upcoming book *Success that Rocks*. He is a man who greets everyone with exuberance, the peace sign, and his favorite blessing, "Rock 'n' Roll!"

facebook.com/Larry.Schardt twitter.com/LarrySchardt

Bestselling author, KATHLEEN SHOOP, holds a PhD in reading education and has more than twenty years of experience in the classroom. She writes historical fiction, women's fiction, and romance. Shoop's novels have garnered various awards in the Independent Publisher Book Awards (IPPY), Eric Hoffer Book Awards, Indie Excellence Awards, Next Generation Indie Book Awards, Readers' Favorite, and the San Francisco Book Festival. Kathleen has been featured in *USA Today* and the *Writer's Guide to 2013*. Her work has appeared in *The Tribune-Review*, four *Chicken Soup for the Soul* books, and *Pittsburgh Parent* magazine. Kathleen coordinates Mindful Writing Retreats and is a regular presenter at conferences for writers. She lives in Oakmont,

Pennsylvania, with her husband and two children. www.kshoop.com, Facebook @Kathleen Shoop.

Dr. DEMI STEVENS, CEO of Year of the Book Press, turns author's writing dreams into successfully published books. She has personally assisted in the production of more than 300 titles by 130 authors, ranging from children's picture books to sizzling romance, award-winning mysteries, and bestselling business books. She holds degrees from West Virginia University, Capital, Northwestern, and Ohio State, and has served on the faculties of Ohio State and Delaware Valley University, and as Director of Paul Smith Library. Many call Demi the "Book Whisperer," but perhaps "Book Midwife" is more appropriate, because literary labor and delivery can be so painful. Each year she coaches a limited number of writers one-on-one through the entire drafting, editing, and publishing process. yotbpress.com

DENISE WEAVER is a freelance writer, a *summa cum laude* graduate of the University of Pittsburgh, and a former library director. With nearly 200 published articles in local and regional magazines, she particularly enjoys interviewing others for personality profiles. She also serves as a copy editor and reader for *Hippocampus Magazine*. A co-founder of Allegheny Regional Festival of Books and a Pennwriters board member, Denise's joy of writing developed from a fifth-grade history class assignment. She had so much fun with the project that she's been playing with words ever since. Having placed as a finalist/honorable mention in several memoir contests, she eagerly awaits her first, first-prize award.

Denise enjoys photography, cooking, and traveling, and once performed on stage at Carnegie Hall. She lives in the beautiful Laurel Highlands of Pennsylvania with her husband and their golden retriever, Murphy O'Malley.

MICHELE SAVAUNAH ZIRKLE, MA, PhD, is a published author, high school teacher and holistic energy practitioner who enjoys sharing innovative ways to break through writing barriers and to live a creative life. She is the author of *Rain No Evil*. In addition to hosting "Life Speaks," on Appalachian Independent Radio, Michele leads meditations and healing events, inspiring participants to live with passion and purpose. Her short stories have appeared in *Mountain Ink Literary Journal* and vignettes in *The Journal of Health* and *Human Experience*. She presents writing workshops for West Virginia Writer's Inc. and Northern Appalachia Writer's Conferences. She is a graduate of Concord University, Marshall Graduate School and The Institute of Metaphysical Humanistic Science.

www.michelezirkle.com   Facebook @ZirksQuirks

Into the Woods (Book 1)
Short stories, poems, essays, music, and one walking meditation. Each piece is unique in tone and genre and the result is that the collection captures the fascinating, frightening, fun, healing, and fantastical wonder of time spent in the woods. The twenty-six contributors who attend Mindful Writers Retreats in the mountains of Ligonier, Pennsylvania, are donating one hundred percent of the proceeds to support the research and work of The Children's Heart Foundation.

Love on the Edge (Book 3)
Experience love's emotional gamut from the authors of Mindful Writers Retreat, sure to bring joy and bliss to your heart any time of year. From love in the time of war... to love at first sight and long walks in the snow... to sparks flying because of nosy neighbors... *Love on the Edge* reveals the essence and evolution of the human need for relationship, written in a time when we're all searching for deeper meaning and connection. Proceeds benefit Allegheny Children's Initiative—Partners For Quality, Inc.